I0642223

George MacDonald

Poems. by George Macdonald, LL. D. Selected by V.D.S. and C.F

George MacDonald

Poems. by George Macdonald, LL. D. Selected by V.D.S. and C.F

ISBN/EAN: 9783744763479

Printed in Europe, USA, Canada, Australia, Japan

Cover: Foto ©Andreas Hilbeck / pixelio.de

More available books at **www.hansebooks.com**

POEMS

BY

GEORGE MACDONALD, LL.D.

SELECTED BY V. D. S. AND C. F.

The lightning and thunder
They go and they come ;
But the stars and the stillness
Are always at home.

NEW YORK
E. P. DUTTON & COMPANY
31 WEST TWENTY-THIRD STREET
1893.

Press of J. J. Little & Co.
Astor Place, New York.

INTRODUCTION.

GEORGE MACDONALD was born at Huntly, Aberdeenshire, Scotland, in 1824. After taking his degree at the University of Aberdeen, he studied theology, and preached for a short time as an Independent minister in Surrey and Sussex. He left the ministry, however, and became a lay member of the Church of England, settling in London and devoting himself to literature. In 1872–73 he lectured in the United States.

Mr. MacDonald is best known as the writer of a number of novels strongly religious in tone. The name of the author of *Wilfrid Cumbermede*, *Annals of a Quiet Neighborhood*, and *Robert Falconer* is familiar to a wide circle of readers. At intervals between 1855 and 1868 four volumes of his poetry were published in England; but American readers have had scant opportunity of becoming acquainted with his verse. It was thought, therefore, that a volume which should include his best work and collect for the first time the charming poems scattered through the novels, would be welcome to many. Most of the poems chosen for this collection are given entire. In a few cases, however, extracts have been taken from a long poem, or omissions made from a shorter one. When this has been done, the poem is marked in the Table of Contents by a star (*). The novel, *Robert Falconer*, contains a number of sonnets or snatches of verse, the authorship of which Mr. MacDonald expressly disclaims. These poems are closely associated with his name ; and several of them are of so great intrinsic value that they have been retained in the present volume. The names of such poems are marked by a dagger (†).

It is perhaps unfair to seek in the verse of an author whose chief work is in prose, an adequate or symmetrical record of his message to the world. The verse of such a man is usually incidental ; it is often the product of youth, when the author has not found the true channel for his energies. Many of Mr. MacDonald's poems are youthful, and the later ones are seldom elaborated with the care given to work to which the author attaches much importance. Technically these verses are often slipshod, diffuse, or abrupt ; and they always represent the occasional overflow of personal emotion rather than the sustained effort to impart truth, characteristic of his prose. Why, then, it may be asked, collect these juvenile or fugitive pieces ? The answer will readily be given by any one who is familiar with the novels of Mr. MacDonald ; for he will perceive the poetic temperament shining out at every turn through the art of the story-teller. The keen and delicate interpretative faculty that renders with loving insight the beauty alike of the commonplace and of the remote ; control of a searching and vivid style and a singular power of suggestion :—these gifts are the gifts of a poet, and they belong emphatically to the prose of Mr. MacDonald.

If we look for them in his poetry we are

not disappointed. We find in it also the same attitude towards life which has proved in Mr. MacDonald's novels helpful to so many. The reader of his novels is first impressed by his intensely religious nature, his habitual reference of all thoughts and acts to a divine source and object. This quality, as might be predicted, is equally marked in his poems. Not that we are to expect from him volumes of religious poetry in the strict sense of the words; but the Scottish bias towards religious contemplation and the profound moral earnestness of the man always lie back of the more superficial gracefulness and fancy which first attract us.

Looking further into his work we find that the prevailing note of Mr. MacDonald's religious thought is its strong hopefulness. He has freed himself from the Scottish gloom and grimness, not by cheerfully ignoring hard facts, but by sternly facing the sternest realities. He is not a shallow optimist; he looks unflinchingly at sin and suffering, at weakness and distortion; he is, indeed, peculiarly sensitive to all forms of evil, as is shown in such a poem as *Contrast;* but he looks beyond these with a manly trust to the deeper, more permanent realities of strength and purity. Poems like *The Lost Soul,* and *What Man is there of You ?* release their author from any charge of superficiality in his philosophy of life.

In their treatment of the spiritual life these poems possess a quality even more noticeable and unique than their courageous honesty of vision ; it is the subtle power with which they delineate certain less obvious phases of nature and experience. Of the morbid analysis into which this subtlety sometimes leads —or sometimes misleads—the poems show no trace. From this he is saved by his wholesomeness of vision on the one hand, and on the other by the fact that with him religious emotion always finds its basis in clear intellectual perception. Such sonnets as those in *A Sonnet Sequence,* or *If Thou Art Tempted by a Thought of Ill,* do not merely reflect and enhance in melodious numbers a pleasing sentiment, but afford real guidance and helpfulness in some of those unrecognized per-

plexities that press upon the. bewildered soul
in its efforts to enter into communion with
the unseen. These perplexities, underlying
as they do our keenest spiritual sorrow and
joy, are seldom touched by religious verse
except in their most obvious aspects; they
are rendered by Mr. MacDonald with sym-
pathetic and accurate penetration; and
therefore is it that they possess an enduring
value. He is one of those authors, more
rare than men of greater genius, who make
less solitary the inmost recesses of the spiritual
life.

From this remoteness and subtlety of subject, it follows that these poems may sometimes seem at first sight a little mystical; but
a straightforward reading will usually destroy
all difficulty. Curiously enough, mysticism
is often in common use only another word
for a certain simplicity of vision. In the
most symbolic utterances of the so-called
mystics, a return to childlike directness of
thought will quickly effect the correspondence
between the spiritual truth and its verbal
form. The long poem, *Somnium Mystici*,

is an example of this class of verse ; and if understood in the most obvious sense it is not difficult to apprehend the quiet beauty with which is depicted the gradual leading to rest in eternal truth of a soul which has passed into the Unseen.

The beauty of this poem is peculiar to its author. Many of Mr. MacDonald's poems, however, suggest other schools of poetry. This fact need in no wise detract from their original value. The significance of an author's work is always easier to understand in the light of his poetic affiliations, especially when the schools whose influence he shows are widely diverse, as in the present case.

The mystical quality in MacDonald's mind suggests his connection with the German school of mystics, and his expressed obligations to Novalis and others shows that he had encouraged this affinity. Translations from Novalis fill a good part of the volume of *Exotics*, and many of MacDonald's own poems reflect with singular exactness the same spirit. Such are *The Day when the Sleepers shall Rise*, and the *Year Song*, poems

that strongly emphasize the spiritual nature
of the whole creation ; and many others
which exhibit the contemplative insight and
restrained ardor of devotion of this German
school.

There is another group of poems which
show by their quaint and rugged grace and
their play of recondite fancy the influence of
our own poets of the seventeenth century,
with whom MacDonald has a great and
avowed sympathy. In some of these poems,
as *Smoke*, and *Consider the Ravens*, there is a
touch of the archaic charm and devotional
spirit that hold us in the best work of saintly
George Herbert, or the fervid though little
known verse of Donne.

Finally, MacDonald shares certain qualities of a third school, more widely known
than either of the preceding—the German
lyrists, headed by Heine. Their pure lyrical
grace and swift apprehension of evanescent
moods are reproduced by Mr. MacDonald
with almost too great facility. The *Picture
Song*, and *Sunset* are instances of this kind of
work ; and, deepened and enriched by the

Scottish love of nature, the same qualities
appear in such lyrics as the *Songs of the Days
and Nights*.

Such, then, are the poetic elements which
combine in Mr. MacDonald : the symbolic
vision of spiritual truth ; a glowing imagina-
tion rich in perceived analogies; and the
clear tenderness of lyrical purity. Add to
these the wide sympathies and moral earnestness of one of the most vital of modern religious teachers, and it is not strange that
one finds in this poet a friendly spirit, and an
interpreter of the deep things of life.

CONTENTS.

CONTENTS.

POEMS FOR CHILDREN.

The lightning and thunder,
  They go and they come ;
But the stars and the stillness
  Are always at home.

POEMS.

A PRAYER FOR THE PAST.

ALL sights and sounds of day and year,
 All groups and forms, each leaf and
  gem,
Are thine, O God, nor will I fear
 To talk to thee of them.

Too great thy heart is to despise ;
 Thy day girds centuries about ;
From things we little call, thine eyes
· See great things looking out.

Therefore the prayerful song I sing
 May come to thee in ordered words ;
Its low-born echo shall not cling ·
 In terror to the chords. .

I think that nothing made is lost,
   That not a moon has ever shone,
That not a cloud my eyes hath crossed,
   But to my soul is gone ;

That all the lost years garnered lie
   In this thy casket, my dim soul ;
And thou wilt, once, the key apply,
   And show the shining whole.

But were they dead in me, they live
   In thee, whose Parable is—Time,
And Worlds, and Forms, and Sounds that give
   Thee back the offered rhyme.

———

THE SMOKE.

LORD, I have laid my heart upon thy altar,·
   But cannot get the wood to burn ;
It hardly flares ere it begins to falter,
   And to the dark return.

Old sap, or night-fallen dew, has damped the
   fuel ;
   In vain my breath would flame provoke ;

Yet see—at every poor attempt's renewal
  To thee ascends the smoke.

'Tis all I have—smoke, failure, foiled en-
    deavor,
  Coldness, and doubt, and palsied lack :
Such as I have I send thee ; perfect Giver,
  Send thou thy lightning back !

THE BURNT-OFFERING.

THRICE happy he, whose heart, each new-
    born night,
When the worn day hath vanished o'er earth's
  brim,
And he hath laid him down in chamber dim,
Straightway begins to tremble and grow
  bright,
And loose faint flashes towards the vaulted
  height
Of the great peace that overshadows him,
Till tongues of fiery hope awake and swim
Thorough his soul, and touch each point with
  light !

Then the great earth a holy altar is,
Upon whose top a sacrifice he lies,
Burning in love's response up to the skies
Whose fire descended first and kindled his :
When slow the flickering flames at length
    expire,
Sleep's ashes only hide the glowing fire.

———

A YEAR SONG.

SIGHING above,
    Rustling below,
Through the woods
The winds go.
Beneath, dead crowds;
Above, life bare;
And the besom winds
Sweep the air.
Heart, leave thy woe ;
Let the dead things go.

Through the brown leaves
Gold stars push ;
A mist of green
Veils the bush.

A YEAR SONG.

Here a twitter,
There a croak !
They are coming—
The spring-folk !
Heart, be not dumb ;
Let the live things come.

Through the beech
The winds go,
With a long speech,
Loud and slow.
The grass is fine,
And soft to lie in ;
The sun doth shine
The blue sky in.
Heart, be alive ;
Let the new things thrive.

Round again !
Here now—
A rimy fruit
On a bare bough !
There the winter,
And the snow ;

And a sighing ever
To fall and go !
Heart, thy hour shall be ;
Thy dead will comfort thee.

———

SUMMONS.

THEY are blind and they are dead ;
   We will wake them as we go;
There are words have not been said ;
There are sounds they do not know.
We will pipe and we will sing,
With the music and the spring,
Set their hearts a wondering.

They are tired of what is old,
We will give it voices new—
For the half hath not been told
Of the Beautiful and True.
Drowsy eyelids shut and sleeping—
Heavy eyes oppressed with weeping !
Flashes through the lashes leaping !

Ye that have a pleasant voice,
Hither come without delay ;
Ye will never have a choice
Like to that ye have to-day :
Round the wide world we will go
Singing through the frost and snow
Till the daisies are in blow.

Ye that cannot pipe or sing,
Ye must also come with speed ;
Ye must come and with you bring
Weighty words and weightier deed.
Helping hands and loving eyes,
These will make them truly wise—
Then will be our Paradise.

OH, THOU OF LITTLE FAITH!

SAD-HEARTED, be at peace : the snow-
drop lies
Buried in sepulchre of ghastly snow ;
But spring is floating up the southern skies,
And darkling the pale snowdrop waits
below.

Let me persuade : in dull December's day
  We scarce believe there is a month of June ;
But up the stairs of April and of May
  The hot sun climbeth to the summer's noon.

Yet hear me : I love God, and half I rest.
  O better ! God loves thee, so all rest thou.
He is our summer, our dim-visioned Best ;—
  And in his heart thy prayer is resting now.

FROM DREAMS OF BLISS.

FROM dreams of bliss shall men awake
  One day, but not to weep :
The dreams remain ; they only break
  The mirror of the sleep.

A SONNET SEQUENCE.

I.

GO thou into thy closet ; shut thy door ;
  And pray to Him in secret : He will
  hear.
  But think not thou, by one wild bound, to
  clear

The numberless ascensions, more and more,
Of starry stairs that must be climbed, before
  Thou comest to the Father's likeness near,
  And bendest down to kiss the feet so dear
That, step by step, their mounting flights
    passed o'er.
Be thou content if on thy weary need
  There falls a sense of showers and of the
    spring ;
  A hope that makes it possible to fling
Sickness aside, and go and do the deed ;
For highest aspiration will not lead
  Unto the calm beyond all questioning.

II.

Hark, hark, a voice amid the quiet intense !
  It is thy Duty waiting thee without.
  Rise from thy knees in hope, the half of
    doubt ;
A hand doth pull thee—it is Providence ;
Open thy door straightway, and get thee
    hence ;
  Go forth into the tumult and the shout ;
  Work, love, with workers, lovers, all about :
Of noise alone is born the inward sense

Of silence ; and from action springs alone
  The inward knowledge of true love and
  faith.
  Then, weary, go thou back with failing
  breath,
And in thy chamber make thy prayer and
  moan.
One day upon *His* bosom, all thine own,
  Thou shalt lie still, embraced in holy death!

III.

And weep not, though the Beautiful decay
  Within thy heart, as daily in thine eyes ;
  Thy heart must have its autumn, its pale
  skies,
Leading, mayhap, to winter's dim dismay.
Yet doubt not.   Beauty doth not pass away;
  Her form departs not, though her body dies.
• Secure beneath the earth the snowdrop lies,
Waiting the spring's young resurrection-day,
Through the kind nurture of the winter cold.
  Nor seek thou by vain effort to revive
  The summer time, when roses were alive;
Do thou thy work—be willing to be old:

Thy sorrow is the husk that doth infold
  A gorgeous June, for which thou need'st
  not strive.

IV.

And should the twilight darken into night,
  And sorrow grow to anguish, be thou strong;
  Thou art in God, and nothing can go wrong
Which a fresh life-pulse cannot set aright.
That thou dost know the darkness, proves the
  light.
  Weep if thou wilt, but weep not all too long ;
  Or weep and work, for work will lead to
  song.
But search thy heart, if, hid from all thy sight,
There lie no cause for beauty's slow decay;
  If for completeness and diviner youth,
  And not for very love, thou seek'st the truth;
If thou hast learned to give thyself away
For love's own sake, not for thyself, I say :
  Were God's love less, the world were lost,
  in sooth.

V.

And do not fear to hope.   Can poet's brain
  More than the Father's heart rich good
  invent ?

Each time we smell the autumn's dying
    scent,
We know the primrose time will come again ;
Not more we hope, nor less would soothe our
    pain.
    Be bounteous in thy faith, for not mis-
    spent
    Is confidence unto the Father lent :
Thy need is sown and rooted for his rain.
His thoughts are as thine own ; nor are his
    ways
    Other than thine, but by their loftier sense
    Of beauty infinite and love intense.
Work on.   One day, beyond all thoughts of
    praise,
A sunny joy will crown thee with its rays ;
    Nor other than thy need, thy recompense.

THE DAY WHEN THE SLEEPERS SHALL RISE.

THE stars are spinning their threads,
    And the clouds are the dust that flies,
And the suns are weaving them up
    For the time when the sleepers shall rise.

The ocean in music rolls,
And gems are turning to eyes,
And the trees are gathering souls
For the time when the sleepers shall rise.

The weepers are learning to smile,
And laughter to glean the sighs,
Burn and bury the care and guile
For the day when the sleepers shall rise.

Oh, the dews and the moths and the daisy-red,
The larks and the glimmers and flows!
The lilies and sparrows and daily bread,
And the something that nobody knows!

PICTURE SONG.

THE waters are rising and flowing
Over the weedy stone—
Over it, over it going :
It is never gone.

Over it joys go sweeping :
'Tis there, the ancient pain ;
Yea, drowned in waves and waves of weeping,
It will rise again.

THE CRIMSON THRONE.

ONCE I sat on a crimson throne,
    And I held the world in fee ;
Below me I heard my brothers moan,
    And I bent me down to see :—

Lovingly bent and looked on them,
    But *I* had no inward pain ;
I sat in the heart of my ruby gem,
    Like a rainbow without the rain.

My throne is vanished : helpless I lie
    At the foot of its broken stair,
And the sorrows of all humanity
    Through my heart make a thoroughfare.

———

THE HURT OF LOVE.

OH, the hurt, the hurt, and the hurt of
        love !
Wherever the sun shines, the waters go.
It hurts the snowdrop, it hurts the dove,
    God on his throne, and man below.

But sun would not shine, nor waters go,
   Snowdrop tremble, nor fair dove moan,
God be on high, nor man below,
   But for love—for the love with its hurt
     alone.

Thou knowest, O Saviour, its hurt and its
     sorrows,
   Didst rescue its joy by the might of thy
     pain :
Lord of all yesterdays, days, and to-morrows,
   Help us love on in the hope of thy gain.

Hurt as it may, love on, love forever ;
   Love for love's sake, like the Father above,
But for whose brave-hearted Son we had never
   Known the sweet hurt of the sorrowful
     love.

DEATH AND BIRTH.

AH ! come in ; I need your aid.
   Tools—you've brought them, as I
     said ?—
The material of your calling—
Stone and lime, dressed, mixed, for walling ?

There, my friend, build up that niche—
That one with the painting rich.—
Yes, you're right ; it is a show
Picture seldom can bestow ;
City palaces and towers,
Terraced gardens, twilight bowers,
Vistas deep through swaying masts,
Pennons flaunting in the blasts.—
Yes, a window you would call it ;
Not the less up you must wall it.
In that niche the dead world lies—
Bury death, and free mine eyes.

There ! 'tis over ; I am dead !
Of the past the broken thread
Only holding in my hand.
O my soul—the merry land !
On my heart, like falling vault,
All the ruining past makes halt ;
Ages I could sit and moan
For the something that is gone.

Haste and pierce the other wall !
Break an opening to the All !
Where ? I care not ; quickest, best.
Kind of window ?   Let that rest :

Who at morning ever lies
Thinking how to ope his eyes?

It were well, of course, to fall
On the thinnest of the wall;—
There is what you call a niche.—
No; this—better far—in which
Stands the Crucifix.　You start?—
Ah, you half-believing heart!
Reverently, the marble cold
In my living arms I fold.
—Thou, the window of the land,
Wouldst not have thy dead form stand
Shutting out the wind and sky,
And the dayspring from on high!
Brother with the rugged crown,
Gently thus I lift thee down.

I will take your tool, and do
What I can to drive it through.
Yes; I have but little skill,
But I have a hearty will.

Stroke on stroke!　The frescoed plaster
Clashes downward, fast and faster.

2

Hark ! I heard an outer stone
Down the rough rock rumbling thrown.
Filters through a sickly beam !
Struggles through an airy stream !
Lo !—the mass is outward flung !
In the universe hath sprung !

See the gold upon the blue,
Where the sun comes blinding through !
See the far-off mountain shine
In the dazzling light divine !
Gloomy world, thy reign is done !
Welcome wind and sky and sun !

AUTUMN SONG.

AUTUMN clouds are flying, flying,
  O'er the waste of blue ;
Summer flowers are dying, dying,
  Late so lovely new.
Laboring wains are slowly rolling
  Home with winter grain ;
Holy bells are slowly tolling
  Over buried men.

Goldener light sets noon a sleeping
  Like an afternoon ;
Colder airs come stealing, creeping,
  From the misty moon ;
And the leaves, of old age dying,
  Earthly hues put on ;
Out on every low wind sighing
  That their day is gone.

Autumn's sun is sinking, sinking
  Down to winter's night ;
And our hearts are thinking, thinking
  Of the cold and blight ;
For our sun is slowly sliding
  Down the hill of might ;
And no moon is softly gliding
  Up the slope of night.

But the vanished corn is lying
  In rich golden glooms ;
In the churchyard, all the sighing
  Is above the tombs ;
And the flowers but wait the blowing
  Of a gentler wind :
Man waits not—through death's door going,
  Man leaves death behind.

Mourn not, then, bright hues that alter ;
    Let the gold turn gray ;
Feet, though feeble, still may falter
    Towards the coming day.
Brother, if thy sorrow lingers
    O'er some withered thing,
Mark at least that Autumn's fingers
    Paint in hues of Spring.

BETTER THINGS.

BETTER to smell the violet cool
    Than sip the glowing wine ;
Better to hark a hidden brook
    Than watch a diamond shine.

Better the love of gentle heart
    Than beauty's favors proud ;
Better the rose's living seed
    Than roses in a crowd.

Better to love in loneliness
    Than bask in love all day ;
Better the fountain in the heart
    Than the fountain by the way.

Better sit at a master's feet
    Than thrill a listening state ;
Better suspect that thou art proud
    Than be sure that thou art great.

Better to walk the realm unseen
    Than watch the hour's event ;
Better the *well-done* at the last
    Than the air with shoutings rent.

Better to have a quiet grief
    Than a hurrying delight ;
Better the twilight of the dawn
    Than the noonday burning bright.

Better a death when work is done
    Than earth's most favored birth ;
Better a child in God's great house
    Than the king of all the earth.

OH, what a unity, to mean them all !—
    The peach-dyed morn, cold stars in
      colder blue
Gazing across upon the sun-dyed west ;
While the cold wind is running o'er the graves.

Green buds, red flowers, brown leaves, and
   ghostly snow;
The grassy hills, breeze-haunted on the brow;
And sandy deserts hung with stinging stars.
Half vanished hangs the moon, with daylight
   sick,
Wan-faced and lost and lonely; daylight
   fades—
Blooms out the pale eternal flower of space,
The opal night, whose odors are gray dreams—
Core of its petal-cup, the radiant moon.
All, all the unnumbered meanings of the
   earth,
Changing with every cloud that passes o'er;
All, all, from rocks slow crumbling in the
   frosts
Of Alpine deserts, isled in stormy air,
To where the pool in warm brown shadows
   sleeps,
The stream, sun-ransomed, dances in the sun;
All, all, from polar seas of jeweled ice
To where she dreams out gorgeous flowers—
   all, all
The unlike children of her single womb—
Oh, my heart labors with infinitude!

All, all the messages that these have borne
To eyes and ears, and watching, listening
    souls ;
And all the kindling cheeks and swelling
    hearts,
That since the first-born, young, attempting
    day,
Have gazed and worshipped !—What a unity,
To mean each one, yet fuse the each in all !
O centre of all forms !   O concord's home !
O world alive in one condensèd world !
O face of Him in whose heart lay concealed
The fountain-thought of all this kingdom of
    heaven !
Lord, thou art infinite, and I am thine !
                    —From *Within and Without.*

SONGS OF THE DAYS AND NIGHTS.

SONGS OF THE SUMMER DAYS.

I.

A GLORY on the chamber wall !
    A glory in the brain !
Triumphant floods of glory fall
    On heath, and wold, and plain.

The earth lies still in hopeless bliss :
  She has, and seeks no more ;
Forgets that days come after this,
  Forgets the days before.

Each ripple waves a flickering fire
  Of gladness, as it runs ;
They laugh and flash, and leap and spire,
  And toss ten thousand suns.

But hark ! low, in the world within,
  One sad Æolian tone :
" Ah ! shall we ever, ever win
  A summer of our own ? "

II.

The morn awakes like brooding dove,
  With outspread wings of gray ;
Her feathery clouds close in above,
  And roof a sober day.

No motion in the deeps of air !
  No trembling in the leaves !
A still contentment everywhere,
  That neither laughs nor grieves !

A film of sheeted silver gray
   Shuts in the ocean's hue ;
White-winged feluccas leave their way
   Behind in gorgeous blue.

Dream on, dream on, O dreamy day !
   Thy very clouds are dreams ;
Yon child is dreaming far away—
   He is not where he seems.

SONG OF THE SUMMER NIGHTS.

THE dreary wind of night is out,
   Homeless and wandering slow ;
O'er pale seas moaning like a doubt,
   It breathes, but will not blow.

It sighs from out the helpless past,
   Where doleful things abide ;
Gray ghosts of dead thought sail aghast
   Across its ebbing tide.

O'er marshy pools it faints and flows,
   All deaf and dumb and blind ;
O'er moor and mountain aimless goes—
   The listless woesome wind !

Nay ! nay !—breathe on, sweet wind of night !
  The sigh is all in me ;
Flow, fan, and blow, with gentle might,
  Until I wake and see.

SONG OF THE AUTUMN DAYS.

AND though the sun be not so warm,
  The future is not lost ;
Both corn and hope, of heart and farm,
  Lie hid from coming frost.

The sombre woods are richly sad ;
  Their leaves are red and gold :
Are thoughts in solemn splendor clad
  Signs that we men grow old ?

Strange odors haunt the doubtful brain
  From fields and days gone by,
And mournful memories again
  Are born, are loved, and die.

The mornings clear, the evenings cool,
  Foretell no wintry wars ;
The day of dying leaves is full ;
  The night of glowing stars.

SONGS OF THE AUTUMN NIGHTS.

I.

O NIGHT, send up the harvest moon
  To walk about the fields,
And make of midnight magic noon
  On lonely tarns and wealds.

In golden ranks, with golden crowns,
  All in the yellow land,
Old solemn kings in rustling gowns,
  The sheaves moon-charmèd stand.

Sky-mirror she, afloat in space,
  Beholds our coming morn :
Her heavenly joy hath such a grace,
  It ripens earthly corn ;

Like some lone saint with upward eyes,
  Lost in the deeps of prayer :
The people still their prayers and sighs,
  And gazing ripen there.

II.

So, like the corn moon-ripened last,
  Would I, weary and gray,
On golden memories ripen fast,
  And ripening pass away.

In an old night so let me die ;
  A slow wind out of doors ;
A waning moon low in the sky ;
  A vapor on the moors ;

A fire just dying in the gloom ;
  Earth haunted all with dreams ;
A sound of waters in the room ;
  A mirror's moony gleams ;

And near me, in the sinking night,
  More thoughts than move in me—
Forgiving wrong, and loving right,
  And waiting till I see.

SONG OF THE WINTER DAYS.

A MORNING clear, with frosty light
  From sunbeams late and low ;

They shine upon the snow so white,
  And shine back from the snow.

Down tusks of ice one drop will go,
  Nor fall : at sunny noon
'Twill hang a diamond—fade, and grow
  An opal for the moon.

And when the bright sad sun is low
  Behind the mountain-dome,
A twilight wind will come and blow
  All round the children's home,

And puff and waft the powdery snow,
  As feet unseen did pass.
But waiting in its bed below
  Green lies the summer grass.

SONG OF THE WINTER NIGHTS.

THE frost weaves ferns and sultry palms
  Across my clouded pane ;
Weaves melodies of ancient psalms
  All through my passive brain.

Quiet ecstasy fills heart and head,
   My father is in the room ;
The very curtains of my bed
   Are filled with sheltering gloom.

The lovely vision melts away ;
   I am a child no more ;
Work rises from the floor of play ;
   Duty is at the door.

But if I face with courage stout
   The labor and the din,
Thou, Lord, wilt let my mind go out,
   My heart with thee stay in.

SONG OF THE SPRING DAYS.

THE sky is smiling over me,
   Hath smiled away the frost ;
With daisies starred the sky-like lea,
   With buds the wood embossed.

Troops of wild flowers gaze at the sky
   Up through the latticed boughs ;
Till comes the green cloud by and by,
   It is not time to house.

Yours is the day, sweet bird—sing on ;
   The winter is forgot ;
Like an ill dream, 'tis over and gone :
   Pain that is past, is not.

Joy that was past, is yet the same :
   If care the summer brings,
'Twill only be another name
   For love that broods, not sings.

SONGS OF THE SPRING NIGHTS.

I.

THE flush of green that dyed the day
   Hath vanished in the moon ;
The strengthened odors float and play
   An unborn, coming tune.

One southern eve like this—the dew
   Had cooled and left the ground ;
The moon hung half-way from the blue,
   No disc, but globèd round ;

Light-leaved acacias, by the door,
   Bathed in the balmy air ;
Clusters of blossomed moonlight bore,
   And breathed a perfume rare ;

Great gold-flakes from the starry sky
　Fell flashing on the deep—
One scent of moist earth floating by
　Did almost make me weep.

II.

Those gorgeous stars were not my own ;
　They made me alien go ;
The mother o'er her head had thrown
　A veil I did not know.

The dusky fields that seaward went,
　The pale, moon-blanchèd glades
Bore flowering grasses, knotted, bent,
　No slender, spear-like blades.

I longed to see the starry host
　Afar in fainter blue ;
But plenteous grass I missed the most,
　With daisies glimmering through.

The common things were not the same—
　I longed across the foam :
From dew-damp earth that odor came—
　I knew the world my home.

III.

The stars are glad in gulfy space—
  Friendly the dark to them !
From day's deep mine, their hiding-place,
  Night wooeth every gem.

A thing for faith 'mid labor's jar,
  When up the day is furled,
Shines in the sky a light afar—
  Perhaps a home-filled world.

Sometimes upon the inner sky
  We catch a doubtful shine :
A mote or star ?   A flash in the eye
  Or jewel of God's mine ?

A star to us, all glimmer and glance
  May swarm with seraphim :
A fancy to our ignorance
  May be a truth to Him.

3

SHADOWS.

A LL things are shadows of thee, Lord ;
　　The sun himself is but a shade ;
My soul is but the shadow of thy word,
　　A candle sun-bedayed.

Diamonds are shadows of the sun ;
　　They drink his rays and show a spark :
My soul some gleams of thy great shine hath
　　　won,
　　And round me slays the dark.

All knowledge is but broken shades—
　　In gulf of dark a wandering horde :
Together rush the parted glory grades—
　　And lo, thy garment, Lord !

My soul, the shadow, still is light,
　　Because the shadow falls from thee ;
I turn, dull candle, to the centre bright,
　　And home flit shadowy.

Shine, shine ; make me thy shadow still—
　　The brighter still the more thy shade ;
My motion be thy lovely, moveless will !
　　My darkness, light delayed !

UNWORTHINESS.

OH ! look not on the heart I bring—
 It is too low and poor ;
I would not have thee love a thing
 Which I can ill endure.

Nor love me for the sake of what
 I would be if I could—
O'er peaks as o'er the marshy flat
 Still soars the sky of good.

See, love, afar, the heavenly man
 The will of God would make ;
The thing I must be when I can,
 Love now, for faith's dear sake.

———

SUNSET.

MY morning rose in laughter,
 A gold and azure day ;
Dull clouds came trooping after,
 Livid and sullen gray.

At noon the rain did batter,
  And it thundered like a hell :
I sighed, It is no matter,
  At night I shall sleep as well.

But I longed with a madness tender
  For an evening like the morn,
That my day might die in splendor,
  Not folded in mist forlorn—

Die like a tone Elysian,
  Like a bee in a cactus-flower,
Like a day-surprisèd vision,
  Like a wind in a summer shower.

Through the vaulted clouds about me
  Broke trembling an azure space—
Was it a dream to flout me,
  Or was it a perfect face ?

The sky and the face together
  Are gone, and the wind blows fell.
But what matters a dream or the weather ?
  At night it will all be well.

For the day of life and labor
  Of ecstasy and pain,
Is only a beaten tabor,
  And I shall not dream again.

But as the old night steals o'er me,
  Deepening till all is dead,
I shall see thee still before me
  Stand with averted head.

And I shall think,   Ah, sorrow !
  The *might* that never was *may !*
The night that has no morrow !
  And the sunset all in gray !

THE PITY OF IT.

A LAS, how easily things go wrong !
    A sigh too much, or a kiss too long,
And there follows a mist and a weeping rain,
And life is never the same again.

Alas, how hardly things go right !
'Tis hard to watch in a summer night,
For the sigh will come, and the kiss will stay,
And the summer night is a winter day.

BETTER TO SIT AT THE WATERS' BIRTH.

BETTER to sit at the waters' birth,
 Than a sea of waves to win ;
To live in the love that floweth forth,
 Than the love that cometh in.

Be thy heart a well of love, my child,
 Flowing, and free, and sure ;
For a cistern of love, though undefiled,
 Keeps not the spirit pure.

REALITY.

THE simplest joys that daily pass
 Grow ecstasies in sleep ;
A wind on heights of waving grass
 In dreams has made me weep.

No wonder then my heart one night
 Was joy-full to the brim :
I was with one whose teaching might
 Had drawn me close to him.

But from a church into the street,
   Came pouring, crowding on,
A troubled throng, with hurrying feet—
   And lo, my friend was gone !

Alone upon a miry road
   I walked a wretched plain ;
Onward without a goal I strode,
   Through mist and drizzling rain.

Low mounds of ruin, ugly pits,
   And brick-fields scarred the globe ;
Those wastes where desolation sits
   Without her ancient robe.

The dreariness, the nothingness,
   Grew worse almost than fear ;
If ever hope was needful bliss,
   Hope sure was needed here !

Was my wish father to the change,
   In some dream-bearing cell ?
Wishes not always fruitless range,
   And sometimes it is well.

I know not. Sudden sank the way !
   Burst in the ocean-waves !

Behold a bright blue-billowed bay,
  Red rocks and sounding caves !

Dreaming I wept.   Awake, I ask—
  Shall Earth in dreams uncouth
Set the old Heavens too hard a task
  To match them with the truth ?

NATURE.

THE sun, like a golden knot on high,
    Gathers the glories of the sky,
And binds them into a shining tent,
Roofing the world with the firmament.
And through the pavilion the rich winds blow,
And through the pavilion the waters go.
And the birds for joy, and the trees for prayer,
Bowing their heads in the sunny air,
And for thoughts, the gently talking springs,
That come from the centre with secret
    things—
All make a music, gentle and strong,
Bound by the earth into one sweet song.
And amidst them all, the mother Earth
Sits with the children of her birth ;

She tendeth them all, as a mother hen
Her little ones round her, twelve or ten :
Oft she sitteth, with hands on knee,
Idle with love for her family.
Go forth to her from the dark and the dust,
And weep beside her, if weep thou must ;
If she may not hold thee to her breast,
Like a weary infant, that cries for rest ;
At least she will press thee to her knee,
And tell a low, sweet tale to thee,
Till the hue to thy cheek, and the light to
    thine eye,
Strength to thy limbs, and courage high
To thy fainting heart, return amain,
And away to work thou goest again.
From the narrow desert, O man of pride,
Come into the house, so high and wide.

THE GREAT SUN BENIGHTED.

THE great sun, benighted,
    May faint from the sky ;
But love, once uplighted,
    Will never more die.

Form, with its brightness,
From eyes will depart :
It walketh, in whiteness,
The halls of the heart.

THE SANGREAL.

How Sir Galahad found and lost the Grail.

GALAHAD was in the night,
And the wood was drear ;
But to men in darksome plight
Radiant things appear.

Wings he heard not floating by,
Heard no heavenly hail ;
But he started with a cry—
Saw the Holy Grail.

Hid from bright, beholding sun,
Hid from moonlight wan—
Lo, from age-long darkness won,
And restored to man !

Three feet off, on cushioned moss,
As if cast away,

Homely wood with carven cross,
　　Rough and rude it lay.

Too much trembling to rise up,
　　Reverent gazed the knight ;
Fearing, daring, towards the cup
　　Stole his hand of might.

But, as if it fled from harm,
　　Sank the holy thing ;
Eager following hand and arm
　　Plunged into a spring.

Oh the thirst ! the water sweet !—
　　Down he lay and quaffed ;
Quaffed and rose up to his feet ;
　　Rose and gayly laughed ;

Fell upon his knees to thank,
　　Loved and lauded there ;
Stretched him on the mossy bank,
　　Fell asleep in prayer ;

Dreamed, and dreaming murmured low
　　Ave, pater, creed ;
When the fir-tops 'gan to glow,
　　Waked and called his steed ;

Drew the girth, and loosed his sword,
   Braced his slackened mail ;
Doubting said : "I dreamed the Lord
   Offered me the Grail."

II.

How Sir Galahad gave up the Quest for the Grail.

Ere the sun had cast his light
   On the water's face,
Firm in saddle rode the knight
   From the holy place ;

Merry songs began to sing,
   Let his matins bide ;
Rode a good hour pondering,
   And was turned aside—

Saying, " I will wisely then
   Cease a hopeless quest
After dream of ancient men—
   Visionary Best !

" Common good than miracle
   Yields a better hold ;

Grail indeed was that fair well
    Full of water cold.

" Not my thirst alone it stilled,
    But my soul it stayed ;
And my heart, with gladness filled,
    Wept and laughed and prayed.

" Hidden church I seek in vale,
    Wood, or lake, no more ;
I shall find a Holy Grail
    Where the need is sore."

III.

How Sir Galahad sought yet again for the
Grail.

On he rode, to succor bound,
    But his faith grew dim :
Wells for thirst he many found,
    Water none for him.

Never more from drinking deep
    Up he rose and laughed ;
Never more a prayerful sleep
    Followed on the draught.

Common water, all they bore,
  Plentifully flowed ;
Quenched his thirst, but ah ! no more
  Eased his bosom's load.

For the *Best* no more he sighed—
  Saw the good askance ;
Life grew vague and poor and wide,
  And his lot a chance.

Then he dreamed through Jesus' hand
  That he drove a nail ;
Woke and cried, " Through every land
  Lord, I seek thy Grail."

IV.

How Sir Galahad found the Grail.

Up the quest again he took,
  Rode through wood and wave ;
Sought in every mossy nook,
  Every hermit cave ;

Sought until the evening red
  Sunk in shadow deep ;

Sought until the moonlight fled ;
   Slept, and sought in sleep.

Where he wandered, seeking, sad,
   Story does not say ;
But at length Sir Galahad
   Found it on a day ;

Took the cup into his hand,
   Held the Grail of joy ;
Carried it about the land,
   Gleesome as a boy ;

Laid his sword where he had found
   Boot for every bale ;
Stuck his spear into the ground ;
   Kept alone the Grail.

V.

How Sir Galahad hid the Grail.

Very still was earth and sky,
   Where in death he lay ;
Oft he said he should not die—
   Would but go away.

When he passed, they reverent sought,
  Where his hand lay prest,
For the cup he bare, they thought,
  Hidden in his breast.

Hope and haste and eager thrill
  Were of none avail :
Hid he held it—deeper still—
  Took with him the Grail.

———

MY friend, if one should tell a homeless
      boy,
"There is your father's house : go in and
  rest ; "
Through every open room the child would go,
Timidly looking for the friendly eye ;
Fearing to touch, scarce daring even to won-
  der
At what he saw, until he found his sire.
But gathered to his bosom, straight he is
The heir of all : he knows it 'midst his tears.
And so with me : not having seen Him yet,
The light rests on me with a heaviness ;

All beauty wears to me a doubtful look ;
A voice is in the wind I do not know ;
A meaning on the face of the high hills
Whose utterance I cannot comprehend.
A something is behind them.   That is God.
These are his words, I doubt not, language
    strange ;
These are the expressions of his shining
    thoughts ;
And he is present, but I find him not.
I have not yet been held close to his heart.
Once in his inner room, and by his eyes
Acknowledged, I shall find my home in these,
'Mid sights familiar as a mother's smiles,
And sounds that never lose love's mystery.
Then they will comfort me.

—From Within and Without.

HARD TIMES.

I AM weary, and very lonely,
    And can but think—think.
If there were some water only
    That a spirit might drink—drink !

4

    And arise,
    With light in the eyes
And a crown of hope on the brow,
    To walk abroad in the strength of gladness,
    Not sit in the house benumbed with sad-
        ness—
    As now !

But, Lord, thy child will be sad—
    As sad as it pleases thee ;
Will sit, not seeking to be glad,
    Till thou bid sadness flee :
        And drawing near
        With a kind " good cheer,"
Awake the life in me.

NOONTIDE.

I LOVE thy skies, thy sunny mists,
    Thy fields, thy mountains hoar,
Thy wind that bloweth where it lists—
    Thy will, I love it more.

I love thy hidden truth to seek
    All round, in sea, on shore ;

The arts whereby like gods we speak—
  Thy will to me is more.

I love thy men and women, Lord,
  The children round thy door ;
Calm thoughts that inward strength afford—
  Thy will, O Lord, is more.

But when thy will my life shall hold,
  Thine to the very core,
The world, which that same will did mould,
  I shall love ten times more.

———

NEW ANGELS.

OF old, with good-will from the skies—
    God's message to them given—
The angels came, a glad surprise,
  And went again to heaven.

But now the angels are grown rare—
  Needed no more as then :
Far lowlier messengers can bear
  God's good-will unto men.

Each year, the snowdrops' pallid dawn
    Breaks from the earth below ;
Till, from the dark exulting drawn,
    The noon of roses glow.

The snowdrops first—the dawning gray ;
    Then out the roses burn !
They speak their word, grow dim—away
    To holy dust return. '

Of oracles were little dearth,
    Should heaven continue dumb ;
From lowliest corners of the earth
    High messages will come.

Since in thy face, redeeming Lord,
    We saw the Father's kind,
We need not much his rarer word—
    Our eyes can read his mind.

———

CONSIDER THE RAVENS.

LORD, according to thy words,
    I have considered thy birds ;
And I find their life good,
And better the better understood :

Sowing neither corn nor wheat,
They have all that they can eat ;
Reaping no more than they sow,
They have all that they can stow ;
Having neither barn nor store,
Hungry again, they eat more.

Considering, I see too that they
Have a busy life, and plenty of play ;
In the earth they dig their bills deep,
And work well, though they do not heap ;
Then to play in the air they are not loath,
And their nests between are better than both.

But this is when there blow no storms,
When berries are plenty in winter, and worms ;
When their feathers are thick, and oil is
    enough
To keep the cold out and the rain off :
If there should come a long hard frost,
Then it looks as thy birds were lost.

But I consider further, and find
A hungry bird has a free mind ;
He is hungry to-day, not to-morrow ;
Steals no comfort, no grief doth borrow ;

This moment is his, thy will hath said it,
The next is nothing till thou hast made it.

The bird has pain, but has no fear,
Which is the worst of any gear ;
When cold and hunger and harm betide him,
He gathers them not to stuff inside him ;
Content with the day's ill he has got,
He waits just, nor haggles with his lot ;
Neither jumbles God's will
With driblets from his own still.

But next I see, in my endeavor,
Thy birds here do not live forever ;
That cold or hunger, sickness or age,
Finishes their earthly stage ;
The rook drops without a stroke,
And never gives another croak ;
Birds lie here, and birds lie there,
With little feathers all astare ;
And in thy own sermon, thou
That the sparrow falls, dost allow.

It shall not cause me any alarm,
For neither so comes the bird to harm,

Seeing our Father, thou hast said,
Is by the sparrow's dying bed ;
Therefore it is a blessed place,
And the sparrow in high grace.
It cometh, therefore, to this, Lord ;
I have considered thy word,
And henceforth will be thy bird

LOWLY SERVICE.

METHOUGHT that in a solemn church
   I stood.
  Its marble acres, worn with knees and feet,
  Lay spread from door to door, from street
    to street.
Midway the form hung high upon the rood
Of Him who gave his life to be our good ;
  Beyond, priests flitted, bowed, and mur-
    mured meet
  Among the candles shining still and sweet:
Men came and went, and worshipped as they
    could—
And still their dust a woman with her
    broom,

Bowed to her work, kept sweeping to the
    door.
Then saw I, slow through all the pillared
    gloom,
Across the church a silent figure come :
    " Daughter," it said, " thou sweepest well
        my floor : "
    " It is the Lord," I cried, and saw no more.

MARY.

SHE sitteth at the Master's feet,
    In motionless employ ;
Her ears, her heart, her soul complete
    Drinks in the tide of joy.

Ah ! who but her the glory knows
    Of life, pure, high, intense,
Whose holy calm breeds awful shows
    Beyond the realm of sense !

In her still ear, his thoughts of grace
    Incarnate are in voice ;
Her thoughts, the people of the place,
    Receive them, and rejoice.

Her eyes, with heavenly reason bright,
　Are on the ground cast low ;
It is his words of truth and light
　That set them shining so.

But see ! a face is at the door
　Whose eyes are not at rest ;
A voice breaks in on wisest lore
　With petulant request.

" Lord," Martha says, " dost thou not care
　She lets me serve alone ?
Tell her to come and take her share."
　Still Mary's eyes shine on.

Calmly she lifts a questioning glance
　To him who calmly heard ;
The merest sign, she'll rise at once,
　Nor wait the uttered word.

The other, standing by the door,
　Waits too what he will say.
His " Martha, Martha " with it bore
　A sense of coming *nay*.

Gently her troubled heart he chid ;
　Rebuked its needless care ;

Methinks her face she turned and hid,
  With shame that bordered prayer.

What needful thing is Mary's choice,
  Nor shall be taken away ?
There is but one,—'tis Jesus' voice ;
  And listening she shall stay.

Oh, joy to every doubting heart,
  Doing the thing it would,
When he, the holy, takes its part,
  And calls its choice the good !

AFTER AN OLD LEGEND.

THE monk was praying in his cell,
  With bowed head praying sore ;
He had been praying on his knees
  For two long hours and more.

When, in the midst, and suddenly,
  His eyes they opened wide ;
And on the ground, behold, he saw
  A man's feet him beside !

And almost to the feet came down
  A garment wove throughout ;
It was not like any he had seen
  In the countries round about.

His eyes he lifted tremblingly
  Until a hand they spied ;
A cut from a chisel there they saw,
  And another scar beside.

Then up they leaped the face to find ;
  His heart gave one wild bound—
One, and stood still with the awful joy—
  He had the Master found !

On his sad ear fell the convent bell :
· 'Twas the hour the poor did wait ;
It was his to dole the daily bread
  That day at the convent gate.

A passion of love within him rose,
  And with duty wrestled strong ;
But the bell kept calling all the time
  With iron merciless tongue.

He gazed like a dog in the Master's eyes—
  He sprang to his feet in strength :

" If I find him not when I come back,
    I shall find him the more at length ! "

He chid his heart, and he fed the poor,
    All at the convent gate ;
Then wearily, oh wearily !
    Went back to be desolate.

His hand on the latch, his head bent low,
    He stood on the door-sill ;
Sad and slow he lifted the latch—
    The Master stood there still !

He said, " I have waited, because my poor
    Had not to wait for thee ;
But the man who doeth my Father's work
    Is never far from me."

Yet, Lord—for thou wouldst have us judge,
    And I will humbly dare—
If the monk had stayed, I do not think
    Thou wouldst have left him there.

I hear from the far-off blessed time
    A sweet defending phrase :
"For the poor always ye have with you,
    But me ye have not always."

A MEDITATION OF ST. ELIGIUS.

Queen Mary one day Jesus sent
  To draw some water, legends tell;
The little boy, obedient,
  Filled full the pitcher from the well.

But as he raised it to his head,
  Heavy, with overflowing rim,
The handle broke, and all was shed
  Upon the stones about the brim.

His cloak upon the ground he laid,
  And in it gathered up the pool;
Obedient there the water stayed,
  And home he bore it plentiful.

Eligius said : " It is not good :
  The hands that all the world control,
Had there been room for wonders, would
  Have made his mother's pitcher whole.

" Yet some few drops for thirsty need,
  An ancient fable even, told
In love of thee, the Truth indeed,
  Like broken pitcher, yet may hold.

" Thy living water I have spilt :
    I thought to bear the pitcher high ;
But on the shining stones of guilt
    I slipped—and there the potsherds lie !

" What will He say whose love will drink
    From poorest cup that love had filled,
If here I sit on Sychar's brink,
    My pitcher broke, thy water spilled ?

" What will they do, I waiting left ?
    They looked to me to bring thy law ;
The well is deep, and, sin-bereft,
    I nothing have wherewith to draw.

" Lord, in the garment of thy flesh
    Thou brought'st the living water first ;
Gather to thee thy truth afresh,
    Afresh to flow for human thirst."

MY CHILD WOKE CRYING FROM HER SLEEP.

MY child woke crying from her sleep :
    I bended o'er her bed,
And soothed her, till in slumber deep
    She from the darkness fled.

And as beside my child I stood,
    A still voice said in me :
" Even thus thy Father, strong and good,
    Is bending over thee."

LORD, HEAR MY DISCONTENT.

LORD, hear my discontent : all blank I
    stand,
A mirror polished by thy hand :
Thy sun's beams flash and flame from me—
I cannot help it : here I stand, there he ;
To one of them I cannot say,
Go, and on yonder water play.
Not one poor ragged daisy can I fashion—
I do not make the words of this my limping
    passion.
If I should say, Now I will think a thought,
Lo ! I must wait, unknowing,
What thought in me is growing,
Until the thing to birth is brought ;
Nor know I then what next will come
From out the gulf of silence dumb ;
I am the door the thing did find
To pass into the general mind ;

I cannot say I think—
I only stand upon the thought-well's brink ;
From darkness to the sun the water bubbles
   up—
I lift it in my cup.
Thou only thinkest—I am thought ;
Me and my thought thou thinkest.   Naught
Am I but as a fountain spout
From which thy water welleth out.
Thou art the only One, the All in all.
—Yet when my soul on thee doth call
And thou dost answer out of everywhere,
I in thy allness have my perfect share.

CONCERNING JESUS.

I.

IF thou hadst been a sculptor, what a race
   Of forms divine had thenceforth filled the
     land !
Methinks I see thee, glorious workman, stand,
Striking a marble window through blind space;
Thy face's reflex on the coming face,

As dawns the stone to statue 'neath thy
    hand—
Body obedient to its soul's command,
Which is thy thought informing it with grace !
So had it been.   But God, who quickeneth
    clay,
Nor turneth it to marble, maketh eyes,
Not shadowy hollows, where no sunbeams
    play,
Would mould his loftiest thought in human
    guise :
Thou didst appear, walking unknown abroad,
God's living sculpture, all-informed of God.

II.

If thou hadst built a temple, how my eye
    Had greedily worshipped, from the low-
    browed crypt
Up to the soaring pinnacles that, tipt
With stars, made signals when the sun drew
    nigh !
Dark caverns in and under ; vivid sky
    Its home and aim ! Say, from the glory slipt,
    And down into the shadows dropt and dipt,
Or reared from darkness up so holy-high ?

5

'Tis man himself, the temple of thy Ghost,
   From hidden origin to hidden fate—
   Foot in the grave, head in blue spaces
      great—
From grave and sky filled with a fighting host.
Fight glooms and glory? or does the glory
      borrow
Strength from the hidden glory of to-morrow?

III.

If thou hadst been a painter, what fresh looks,
   What outbursts of pent glories, what new
      grace
   Had shone upon us from the great world's
      face !
How had we read, as in new-languaged books,
Clear love of God in loneliest, shiest nooks !
   A lily, if thy hand its form did trace,
   Had plainly been God's child, of lower
      race ;—
How strong the hills, how sweet the grassy
      brooks !
To thee all nature open lay, and bare,
   Because thy soul was nature's inner side ;
   Clear as the world on the dawn's golden tide,

Its vast idea in thy soul did rise ;
Thine was the earth, thine all her meanings
   rare—
  The ideal Man, with the eternal eyes !

IV.

If thou hadst built some mighty instrument,
  And set thee down to utter ordered sound,
  Whose faithful billows, from thy hands un-
    bound,
Breaking in light, against our spirits went,
And caught, and bore above this earthly tent
  The far-strayed back to their prime natal
    ground,
  Where all roots fast in harmony are found,
And God sits thinking out a pure concent ;
If—ah ! how easy that had been for thee !
  Our broken music thou must first restore—
A harder task than think thine own out free ;
  But till thou hast done it, no divinest score,
Though rendered by thine own angelic choir,
Could lift a human soul from foulest mire.

V.

Our ears thou openedst, mad'st our eyes to see.
  All they who work in stone or color fair,

Or build up temples of the quarried air,
Which we call music, scholars are of thee.
Henceforth in might of such the earth shall be
  Truth's temple-theatre, where she shall
    wear
  All forms of revelation, and they bear
Tapers in acolyte humility.
O Master-maker ! thy exultant art
  Goes forth in making makers. Pictures ?
    No ;
  But painters, who in love and truth shall
    show
Glad secrets from thy God's rejoicing heart.
All-unforetold, green grass and corn up start,
  When through dead sands thy living waters
    go.

VI.

From the beginning good and fair are one,
  But men the beauty from the truth will
    part,
  And, though the truth is ever beauty's heart,
After the beauty will, short-breathèd, run,
And the indwelling truth deny and shun.
  Therefore in cottage, synagogue, and mart,

Thy thoughts came forth in common
  speech, not art ;
With voice and eye in Jewish Babylon
Thou taughtest—not with pen or carved stone,
  Nor in thy hand the trembling wires did
    take ;
  Thou of the truth not less than all wouldst
    make ;
For her sake even her forms thou didst dis-
  own :
Ere beauty cause the word of truth to fail,
Thy light behind shall burn the broidered veil.

VII.

Holy of holies !—Lord, let me come nigh !
  For, Lord, thy body is the shining veil
  By which I look on God and am not pale.
Forgive me, if in these poor verses lie
Mean thoughts, for see, the thinker is not
  high.
  But were my song as loud as saints' all-hail,
  As pure as prophet's cry of warning wail,
As holy as thy mother's ecstasy,
I know a better thing—for love or ruth,
To my weak heart a little child to take.

Nor thoughts nor feelings, art nor wisdom
  seal
The man who at thy table bread shall break.
  Thy praise was not that thou didst know,
    or feel,
Or show, or love, but that thou didst the
  truth.

———

IF I HIM BUT HAVE.

IF I Him but have,
  If he be but mine,
If my heart, hence to the grave,
  Ne'er forgets his love divine—
Know I naught of sadness,
Feel I naught but worship, love, and glad-
  ness.

If I Him but have,
  Glad with all I part ;
Follow on my pilgrim staff
  My Lord only, with true heart :
Leave them, nothing saying,
On broad, bright, and crowded highways
  straying.

If I Him but have,
  Glad I fall asleep ;
Aye the flood that his heart gave
  Strength within my heart shall keep ;
And with soft compelling
Make it tender, through and through it
  swelling.

If I Him but have,
  Mine the world I hail !
Glad as cherub smiling grave,
  Holding back the Virgin's veil.
Sunk and lost in seeing,
Earthly cares have died from all my being.

Where I have but Him
  Is my Fatherland,
And all gifts and graces come
  Heritage into my hand :
Brothers long deplored
I in his disciples find restored.
                    —From *Novalis.*

THE SHADOWS.

MY little boy, with smooth, fair cheeks,
And dreamy, large, brown eyes,
Not often, little wisehead, speaks,
But what he hears, he tries.

"God is not only in the sky"—
His sister said one day;
For she was sometimes pleased to cry
Like Wisdom in the way:

"He's in this room." Dreaming yet clear,
His eyes went round for God.
Vain all to look, vain all to peer !—
His wits are quite abroad.

"He is not here, mamma? No, no;
I do not see him at all.
"He's not the shadows, is he?" So ·
His doubtful accents fall—

Fall on my heart—no babble mere !
They rouse both love and shame :
But for the loneliness and fear,
I still had thought the same.

Oh ! sometimes, ere the morning break.
  And home the shadows flee,
In my dim room even yet I take
  The shadows, Lord, for thee !

CONTRAST.

SOME men there are who cannot spare
  A single tear until they feel
  The last cold pressure, and the heel
Is stamped upon the outmost layer.

And, waking, some will sigh to think
  The clouds have borrowed winter's wing—
  Sad winter, when the grasses spring
No more about the fountain's brink.

And some would call me coward—fool :
  I lay a claim to better blood—
  But yet a heap of idle mud
·Hath power to make me sorrowful.

HUNGER FOR RIGHTEOUSNESS.

FATHER, I cry to thee for bread,
    With hungered longing, eager prayer;
Thou hear'st and givest me instead
    More hunger and a half despair.

O Lord ! how long ? My days decline,
    My youth is lapped in memories old,
I need not bread alone, but wine—
    See, cup and hand to thee I hold.

And yet thou givest : thanks, O Lord,
    That still my heart with hunger faints !
The day will come when at thy board
    I sit forgetting all my plaints.

If rain must come and winds must blow,
    And I pore long o'er dim-seen chart,
Yet, Lord, let not the hunger go,
    And keep the faintness at my heart.

THE LOST SOUL.

SEND your eyes across the gray,
   By my finger-point away,
Through the fumy, thickened air.
Beyond the air, you see the dark ;
Beyond the dark, the dawning day :
On its horizon, pray you, mark
Something like a ruined heap
Of worlds half uncreated, that go back
Slow to the awful deep
Of nothingness, bare being's lack,
Down all the stairs whereby they rose
Up to harmonious life, and law's repose :
On its surface, lone and bare,
Shapeless as a dumb despair,
Formless, nameless, something lies :
Can the vision in your eyes
Its idea recognize ?

   A poor lost soul it is, alack !—
Half he lived some ages back.
But with half-way opened eyes,
Thinking him already wise,

Down he sat and wrote a book—
Drew his life into a nook,
And out of it would not arise
To read the letters dim,
The sayings dark upon his walls ;
He said they were but chance-led scrawls,
Or at best no use to him.
He had a lamp for reading these—
He trimmed it as he sat at ease,
Sat at ease and would not look—
Trimmed it down to one faint spark ;
It went out and left him dark.
Let me try if he will hear
Spirit words with spirit ear.

    Motionless thing ! who once
Like him who cries to thee,
Hadst thy place in the mystic dance
From the doors of the far eternity,—
A place in the dance of thy radiant peers,
Issuing ever, with feet that glance
To the joyous law that binds the free,
To the clang of the crystal spheres !
O heart for love ! O thirst to drink
From the wells that feed the sea !

O hands of truth—a golden link
'Twixt mine and the Father's knee !
O eyes to see !   O soul to think !
O life, the brother of me !
Has the Infinite sucked back all
The individual life it gave ?
Boots it nothing to cry and call ?
Is thy form an empty grave ?

It heareth not, brothers, we need not tarry!
Sounds no sense to its ear will carry ;
Sting it with words, it will never shrink ;
It cannot repent, it will not think.
Hath God forgotten it, alas !
Lost in eternity's lumber-room ?
Will the wind of his breathing never pass
Over it through the insensate gloom ?
Like a frost-killed bud on a tombstone curled,
Crumbling it lies on its crumbling world,
Sightless and soundless, with never a cry,
In the hell of its own vacuity !

See, see yon angel cross our flight,
When the thunder-vapors loom—
From his upcast pinions flashing the light
Of some outbreaking doom !

—Up, brothers ! away ! a storm is nigh !
Smite we the wing up a steeper sky !
What matters the hail or the clashing winds—
The thunder that buffets, the lightning that
    blinds ?
We know by the tempests we do not lie
Dead in the pits of eternity !

ANTIPHONY.

DAYLIGHT fades away.
    Is the Lord at hand,
In the shadows gray
    Stealing on the land ?

Gently from the east
    Come the shadows gray ;
But our lowly priest
    Nearer is than they.

    It is darkness quite.
      Is the Lord at hand,
    In the cloak of night
      Stolen upon the land ?

But I see no night,
  For my Lord is here ;
With him dark is light,
  With him far is near.

     List ! the cock's awake.
       Is the Lord at hand ?
     Cometh he to make
       Light in all the land ?

Long ago he made
  Morning in my heart ;
Long ago he bade
  Shadowy things depart.

     Lo ! the dawning hill !
       Is the Lord at hand,
     Come to scatter ill,
       Ruling in the land ?

He hath scattered ill,
  Ruling in my mind.
Growing to his will,
  Freedom comes, I find.

     We will watch all day,
       Lest the Lord should come ;

All night waking stay,
  In the darkness dumb.

I will work all day,
  For the Lord hath come;
Down my head will lay,
  All night glad and dumb.

      For we know not when
        Christ may be at hand;
      But we know that then
        Joy is in the land.

For I know that where
  Christ hath come again,
Quietness without care
  Dwelleth in his men.

HALF-SIGHT.

O LORD! if on the wind at cool of day,
    I heard one whispered word of mighty
      grace;
If through the darkness as in bed I lay,
    But once had come a hand upon my face;

If but one sign that might not be mistook,
   Had ever been, since first thy face I sought,
I should not now be doubting on a book,
   But serving thee with burning heart and
     thought.

So dreams that heart. But to my heart I say,
   Turning my face to front the dark and wind:
Such signs had only barred anew his way
   Into thee, longing heart, thee, wildered
     mind.

They asked the very Way, where lies the way;
   The very Son, where is the Father's face ;
How he could show himself, if not in clay,
   Who was the Lord of spirit, form, and
     space ?

My being, Lord, will nevermore be whole
   Until thou come behind mine ears and eyes,
Enter and fill the temple of my soul
   With perfect contact—such a sweet sur-
     prise—

Such presence as, before it met the view,
   The prophet-fancy could not once foresee,
6

Though every corner of the temple knew
　By very emptiness its need of thee.

When I keep *all* thy words—no favored
　　some—
　Heedless of worldly winds or judgment's
　　tide,
Then, Jesus, thou wilt with thy Father come—
　O ended prayers !—and in my soul abide.

Ah ! long delay ! ah ! cunning, creeping sin !
　I shall but fail and cease at length to try.
O Jesus ! though thou art not yet come in,
　Knock at my window as thou passest by.

———

THE DISCIPLE.

I.

I KNEEL.　But all my soul is dumb
　　With hopeless misery :
Is *he* a friend who will not come,
　Whose face I may not see ?

It is not fear of broken laws,
　Or judge's damning word ;

It is a lonely pain, because
   I call and am not heard.

A cry where no man is to hear,
   Doubles the lonely pain ;
Returns in silence on the ear,
   In torture on the brain.

No look of love a smile can bring,
   No kiss wile back the breath
To cold lips : I no answer wring
   From this great face of death.

II.

Yet sometimes when the agony
   Dies of its own excess,
Unhoped repose descends on me,
   A reign of gentleness ;

A sense of bounty and of grace,
   A calm within my breast,
As if the shadow of his face
   Did fall on me and rest.

'Tis God, I say, and cry no more—
   Upraised, with strength to stand

And wait unwearied at the door,
   Till comes an opening hand.

III.

But is my will alive, awake ?
   The one God will not heed,
If in my lips or hands I take
   A half-word or half-deed.

Day after day I sit and dream
   Amazed in outwardness ;
The powers of things that only seem,
   The things that are oppress ;

Till in my soul some discord sounds,
   Till sinks some yawning lack ;
I turn me from life's rippling rounds,
   And unto thee come back.

IV.

Years have passed o'er my broken plan
   To picture out a strife,
Where ancient Death, in horror wan,
   Faced young and fearing Life.

More of the tale I tell not so—
    But for myself would say :
My heart is quiet with what I know,
    With what I hope is gay.

And where I cannot set my faith,
    Unknowing or unwise,
I say, " If this be what *he* saith,
    Here hidden treasure lies."

Through years gone by since thus I strove,
    Thus shadowed out my strife,
While at my history I wove,
    Thou didst weave in the life.

Through poverty that had no lack,
    For friends divinely good ;
Through pain that not too long did rack,
    Through love that understood ;

Through light that taught me what to hold,
    And what to cast away ;
Through thy forgiveness manifold,
    And things I cannot say,

Here thou hast brought me—able now
    To kiss thy garment's hem,

Entirely to thy will to bow,
   And trust thee even for them,

Who, lost in darkness, in the mire,
   With ill-contented feet,
Walk trailing loose their white attire,
   For the sapphire-floor unmeet.

Lord Jesus Christ, I know not how—
   With this blue air, blue sea,
This yellow sand, that grassy brow,
   All isolating me—

My words to thy heart should draw near,
   My thoughts be heard by thee ;
But he who made the ear must hear,
   Who made the eye, must see.

Thou mad'st the hand with which I write,
   That sun descending slow
Through rosy gates, that purple light
   On waves that shoreward go,

Bowing their heads in golden spray
   As if thy foot were near :
I think I know thee, Lord, to-day,
   Have known thee many a year.

I know thy Father—thine and mine—
  Thus thy great word doth go :
If thy great word the words combine,
  I will not say, *Not so.*

Lord, thou hast much to make me yet—
  A feeble infant still :
Thy thoughts, Lord, in my bosom set,
  Fulfil me of thy will,

Even of thy truth, both in and out,
  That so I question free :
The man that feareth, Lord, to doubt,
  In that fear doubteth thee.

———

TO S. F. S.

THEY say that lonely sorrows do not
  chance.
It may be true ; one thing I think I know :
New sorrow joins a gliding funeral slow
With less jar than it shocks a merry dance.
But if griefs troop, why, joy doth joy enhance

As often, and the balance levels so.
If quick to see flowers by the wayside blow,
As quick to feel the lurking thorns that lance
The foot that walketh naked in the way,—
Blest by the lily, white from toils and fears,
Oftener than wounded by the thistle-spears,
We should walk upright, bold, and earnest-
    gay,
And when the last night closed on the last
    day,
Should sleep like one that far-off music hears.

PRAYER.

WE doubt the word that tells us : Ask,
    And ye shall have your prayer ;
We turn our thoughts as to a task,
    With will constrained and rare.

And yet we have ; these scanty prayers
    Yield gold without alloy :
O God ! but he that trusts and dares
    Must have a boundless joy.

WHAT MAN IS THERE OF YOU ?

THE homely words, how often read !
   How seldom fully known !
Which father of you, asked for bread,
   Would give his child a stone ?

How oft has bitter tear been shed,
   And heaved how many a groan,
Because thou wouldst not give for bread
   The thing that was a stone !

How oft the child thou wouldst have fed
   Thy gift away has thrown !
He prayed, thou heardst and gav'st the bread ;
   He cried—It is a stone !

Lord, if I ask in doubt and dread
   Lest I be left to moan—
I am the man who, asked for bread,
   Would give his son a stone.

THE WOMAN WHOM SATAN HAD BOUND.

FOR eighteen years, she, patient soul,
   Her eyes hath graveward sent ;
All vain for her the starry pole,
   She is so bowed and bent.

What mighty words !   Who can be near ?
   What tenderness of hands !
Oh ! is it strength, or fancy mere ?
   New hope, or breaking bands ?

The pent life rushes swift along
   Channels it used to know ;
And up, amidst the wondering throng,
   She rises firm and slow—

To bend again in grateful awe—
   Will, power no more at strife—
In homage to the living Law
   Who gives her back her life.

Uplifter of the drooping head !
   Unbinder of the bound !
Thou seest our sore-burdenèd
   Bend hopeless to the ground.

What if they see thee not, nor cry—
  Thou watchest for the hour
To raise the forward-beaming eye,
  To wake the slumbering power.

I see thee wipe the stains of time
  From off the withered face ;
Lift up thy bowed old men, in prime
  Of youthful manhood's grace.

Like summer days from winter's tomb,
  Arise thy women fair ;
Old age, a shadow, not a doom,
  Lo ! is not anywhere.

All ills of life shall melt away
  As melts a cureless woe,
When, by the dawning of the day
  Surprised, the dream must go.

I think thou, Lord, wilt hear me too,
  Whate'er the needful cure ;
The great best only thou wilt do,
  And hoping I endure.

WIND OF GOD.

O WIND of God, that blowest in the mind,
  Blow, blow, and wake the gentle spring
    in me ;
Blow, swifter blow, a strong warm summer
  wind,
Till all the flowers with eyes come out to see;
Blow till the fruit hangs red on every tree,
And our high-soaring song-lark meets thy
  dove—
High the imperfect soars, descends the per-
  fect love.

Blow not the less, though winter cometh then;
Blow, wind of God, blow hither changes keen ;
Let the spring creep into the ground again,
The flowers close all their eyes, not to be seen;
All lives in thee that ever once hath been :
Blow, fill my upper air with icy storms ;
Breathe cold, O wind of God, and kill my
  canker-worms.

UP IN THE TREE.

WHAT would you see, if I took you up
    My little aerie-stair?
You would see the sky like a clear blue cup
    Turned upside down in the air.

What would do, up my aerie-stair,
    In my little nest on the tree?
My child with cries would trouble the air,
    To get what she could but see.

What would you get in the top of the tree,
    For all your crying and grief?
Not a star would you clutch of all you see—
    You could only gather a leaf.

But when you had lost your greedy grief,
    Content to see from afar,
You would find in your hand a withering leaf,
    In your heart a shining star.

A CHRISTMAS CAROL.

BABE Jesus lay in Mary's lap ;
  The sun shone on his hair ;
And this was how she saw, mayhap,
  The crown already there.

For she sang : " Sleep on, my little king ;
  Bad Herod dares not come ;
Before thee, sleeping, holy thing,
  The wild winds would be dumb.

" I kiss thy hands, I kiss thy feet,
  My child, so long desired ;
Thy hands shall never be soiled, my sweet;
  Thy feet shall never be tired.

" For thou art the king of men, my son ;
  Thy crown I see it plain ;
And men shall worship thee, every one,
  And cry Glory ! Amen."

Babe Jesus opened his eyes so wide !
  At Mary looked her Lord.
And Mary stinted her song and sighed.
  Babe Jesus said never a word.

LUTHER'S CHRISTMAS HYMN.

FROM heaven above I come to you
  To bring a story good and new :
Of goodly news so much I bring—
I cannot help it, I must sing.

To you a child is come this morn,
A child of holy maiden born ;
A little babe, so sweet and mild—
It is a joy to see the child.

'Tis little Jesus, whom we need
Us out of sadness all to lead :
He will himself our Saviour be,
And from all sinning set us free.

Take heed, my heart. Be lowly. So
Thou seest him lie in manger low :
That is the baby sweet and mild ;
That is the little Jesus-child.

Ah, Lord ! the maker of us all !
How hast thou grown so poor and small,
That there thou liest on withered grass—
The supper of the ox and ass ?

Ah, little Jesus! lay thy head
Down in a soft, white, little bed,
That waits thee in this heart of mine,
And then this heart is always thine.

Such gladness in my heart would make
Me dance and sing for thy sweet sake.
Glory to God in highest heaven,
For he his Son to us hath given!

EARTH'S CONSOLATION, WHY SO SLOW?

EARTH'S Consolation, why so slow?
    Thy inn is ready long ago;
Each lifts to thee his hungering eyes,
And open to thy blessing lies.

O Father, pour it forth with might;
Out of thine arms, oh! yield him quite;
Peace only, love, sweet shame I know
Kept him from coming long ago.

Ah! make him leave thee for our arm,
Thy breath yet breathing on us warm;

The heavy clouds around him throw,
And let him downward hither so.

In cooling streams send him to us ;
In flames let him glow tremulous ;
In air, oil, sound, and dew, oh ! let
Him earth's bulk interpenetrate.

So shall the holy fight be fought ;
So come the rage of hell to naught ;
And, ever blooming, young as then,
Out comes old Paradise again.

Earth stirs once more, grows green and live ;
Full of the spirit, all things strive
To clasp with love the Saviour guest,
And offer him the mother's breast.

The winter fails ; a year new-born
Stands by the manger's altar-horn ;
'Tis the first year of that new earth
Which this child claims in right of birth.

Our eyes they see the Saviour well,
Yet in them doth the Saviour dwell ;
With flowers his head is wreathed about,
From which himself looks gracious out.

7

He is the star ; he is the sun ;
Life's well that evermore will run ;
From herb and stone, light, sea's expanse,
Glimmers his childish countenance.

His childlike labor things to mend,
His ardent love will never end ;
He nestles, with unconscious art,
Divinely fast to every heart.

To us a God, to himself a child,
He loves us all, self-undefiled ;
Becomes our drink, becomes our food—
His dearest thanks, a heart that's good.

The misery grows yet more and more ;
A gloomy grief afflicts us sore ;
Keep him no longer, Father ; thus
He will come home again with us.

　　　　　　　　　　—From *Novalis.*

SOMNIUM MYSTICI.

A MICROCOSM IN TERZA RIMA.

I.

QUIET I lay at last, and knew no more
 Whether I breathed or not—so worn
  I lay
With the death-struggle. What was yet before
 Neither I met, nor turned from it away.
My only conscious being was the deep rest
 Of torture dead—gone with the bygone day.
And long I could have lingered—all but blest,
 In that slow dreamy pause. But came a
  sound
As of a door that opened—in the west
 Somewhere I thought it was. The noise
  unbound
The sleep from off my eyelids, and they rose,
 And I looked forth. And looking, straight
  I found
It was my chamber door that did unclose,
 Whence a tall form up to my bedside drew—
Grand, silent, bending almost with repose ;
 And when I saw his countenance I knew

That I was lying in my chamber dead ;
　For this my brother—brothers such are
　　few—
That now to greet me bowed his kingly head,
　Had, many years agone, like holy dove
Returning, from his friends and kindred sped,
　And, leaving memories of mournful love,
Passed vanishing behind the unseen veil ;
　And though I loved him, all high words
　　above,
Not for his loss then did I weep or wail,
　Knowing that here we live but in a tent,
And that our house is yonder, without fail :
　Now eager, up to meet him, slow I bent—
I too was dead, so might the dead embrace.
　The dear, long-fingered hand silent he lent,
And lifted me.　I was in feeble case,
　But growing stronger, stood upon the floor ;
Then turned and once regarded my dead face,
　With curious eyes : its brow contentment
　　bore—
But I had done with it.　I turned away,
　And seeing my brother by the open door,
Followed him out into the night blue-gray.
　The houses stood up hard in limpid air,

The moon hung in the heavens in half decay,
And all the world to my bare feet lay bare.

II.

Now I had suffered in my life—as they
    Suffer who still by slow years younger grow,
And feel the false, vain self dropping away,
    Which, born of greed and fear, had gath-
    ered slow,
Darkening the angel-self that, evermore,
    Where no vain phantom in or out shall go,
Moveless beholds the Father—stands before
    The throne of revelation, waiting there,
With wings low-drooping on the sapphire-
    floor,
    Until they find the Father's ideal fair,
And are themselves at last : not one small
    thorn
    Shall needless any pilgrim's garments tear;
And thus to speak of suffering I would scorn,
    But for a marvellous thing that next be-
    fell :—
Sudden I grew aware I was new-born ;
    All pain had vanished in the absorbing
    swell

Of some exalting peace that was my own :
   As the moon dwelt in heaven, did calmness
    dwell
At home in me, essential.   The earth's moan
   Lay all behind.   Had I then lost my part
In human griefs—dear part with them that
    groan ?
   " 'Tis weariness," I said ; but with a start
That set it trembling, and yet brake it not,
   I found the peace was love.   Oh, my rich
    heart !
For every time I caught a glimmering spot
   Of window-pane—" There, in that silent
    room,"
. I thought, " sleeps one in whose expanding
    lot
   I have a part : "—I cared for that one,
    whom
I saw not, had not seen, and might not see.
   After the love crept prone its shadow-
    gloom ;
But instant a mightier love arose in me—
   As in an ocean a single wave might swell—
And heaved the shadow to the centre : we
   Had called it prayer, before on sleep I fell.

It sank, and left my sea in holy calm :
I gave each man to God, and all was well.
On my left side my brother, with one palm
Stretched open out, level before him, went
One step in front of me. A heavenly balm
Flowed from his presence—ere long with
sadness blent.

III.

Nor softest murmur through the city crept,
Nor one lone word my brother to me had
spoken ;
But when beyond the city-gate we stept,
I knew the silent spell would soon be bro-
ken.
A cool night wind came whispering : through
and through
It soft baptized me with the pledge and
token
Of that sweet spirit-wind which blows and
blew,
And fans the human world since evermore.
The very grass, cool to my feet, I knew
To be love also, and with the love I bore

To hold far sympathy, silent and sweet,
   As having known the secret from of yore.
And now my heart was eager all to meet
   The eyes and voice of him who onward led,
When he stood sudden, and, with arrested
    feet,
   I also.   Like a half-sunned orb, his head
Slow turned the bright side : Lord, the
    brother-smile
   That ancient human glory on me shed,
In which thou clothéd camest forth to wile
   Unto thy bosom every laboring soul,
And its dividing passions to beguile
   To a glad winsome death, and on them roll
. The blessed stone of the Holy Sepulchre.
   "Brother," he said, "thou art like me now
    —whole
And sound and well ; for the keen pain, and
    stir
   Uneasy, and the grief that came to us all,
In that we knew not how the wine and myrrh
   Could ever from the vinegar and gall
Be parted—are deep sunk, yea drowned in
    God ;
   And yet the past not folded in a pall,

But breathed upon, like Aaron's withered rod,
  By a sweet light that brings the blossoms
    through—
Showing in dreariest paths that men have
    trod,
  Another's foot-prints, spotted of crimson
    hue,
Still on before, wherever theirs did wend ;
  Yea, through the desert leading—of thyme
    and rue,
The desert souls in which the lions rend
  And roar—the passionate who, to be blest,
Ravin as bears, and do not gain their end,
  Because that, save in God, can be no rest."

IV.

Something my brother said to me like this—
  But how unlike it also, think, I pray :
His eyes were music, and his smile a kiss ;
  Himself the word, his speech was but a ray
In the clear nimbus that with verity
  Of absolute utterance made a home-born
    day
Of truth about him, lamping solemnly.

And when he paused, there came a swift
repose,
Too high, too still to be called ecstasy—
A purple silence, lanced through in the
close
By such keen thought, it grew, suddenly
smiling,
Sheen silver with a heart of burning rose.
It was a glory full of reconciling,
Of perfect faithfulness, and love, and pain;
Of tenderness, and care, and mother-wiling
Back to the bosom of a speechless gain.

V.

I cannot tell how long we joyous talked,
For from my sense old time had vanished
quite,
Space dim remaining—for onward still we
walked.
No sun arose to blot the pale, still night—
Still as the night of some great spongy stone
That turns but once an age betwixt the
light
And the huge shadows from its own bulk
thrown ;—

Long as that night to me—before whose
  face
Visions so many slid, and veils were blown
  Aside from the vague vast of Isis' grace.
Innumerous thoughts did throng that infinite
  hour,
  And in me hopes did hopes unceasing
  chase,
For I was all responsive to his power.
  I saw my friends weep, wept, and let them
  weep :
I saw the dawn of the grief-nurtured flower,
  And the gardener Jesus watching—in their
  sleep
Wiping their tears with the napkin he had laid
  Wrapped by itself when he climbed Hades
  steep.
Faith found it easy there ; but undismayed
I also saw the abortive monsters nursed
In slimy coverts—the rich man that preyed,
  And the poor man that ground his neigh-
  bor worst ;
Yea, all the human chaos, wild and waste,
  Where what high God for evermore hath
  cursed,

To madder wallowing is stung and chased
  By dim recallings of the good forgot.
But he that will believe shall not make haste;
  For God may shut into a seed no jot
Less than an æon ; give a world that lay
  Wombed in its sun, a molten, unorbed clot,
One moment from the red rim to spin away,
  Librating—ages to roll on weary wheel,
Ere home it come—fulfilled its year-full day :
  Who in the chiliad sees the day, shall feel
No anxious heart, shall lift no trembling hand;
  But, keen-dividing as the sword of steel
That from His mouth went forth in Patmos-
    land,
  Shall ever hope, and, to his labor bent,
The Father's will shall, doing, understand.
  So spake my brother as we onward went :
I drank his words, as dew the summer-lea,
  Till faith had almost blossomed in content.
We came at last upon a lonesome sea.

VI.

Right onward still he went, I following,
  Out on the water.   But the water, lo !

Like a thin sheet of glass, lay vanishing ;
The starry host in glorious two-fold show
Shone up, shone down ! and soon as I saw
    this
A quivering dread thorough my heart did go:
Unstayed, I walked athwart a twin abyss,
    A hollow sphere of blue ! nor floor was
    found
Of seeing eye, only the foot met the kiss
    Of the cool water, lightly crisping round
The edges of the footsteps !   Terror froze
    My fallen eyelids.   But again the sound
Of my guide's voice on the still air arose.
    " Hast thou forgotten that we walk by faith ?
For keenest sight but multiplies the shows.
    Lift up thine eyelids ; take a valiant breath;
Fearful, dare yet the terror in God's name ;
    Step wider ; trust the invisible. Can Death
Avail no more to hearten up thy flame ? "
I trembled, but I opened wide mine eyes,
And strode on the invisible sea.   The same
    High moment vanished all my cowardice,
And God was with me ; the well-pleasèd stars
    Threw quivering smiles across the gulfy
    skies.

And the aurora flashed great scimitars
  From north to zenith ; and once more my
    guide
Full turned with blessed face. No prison-bars
  Latticed across a soul I there descried,
No weather-stains of grief ; quiet age-long
  Brooded upon his forehead clear and wide ;
Yet from that face a pang shot, vivid and strong,
  Into my heart ; for though I saw him stand
Close to me in the void as one in a throng,
  Yet on the border of some nameless land
He stood afar ; a still-eyed mystery
  Caught him whole worlds away. Though
    in my hand
His hand I held, and, gazing earnestly,
  Searched in his countenance, as in a mine,
For jewels of contentment, satisfy
  My heart I could not. Seeming to divine
My hidden trouble, gently he stooped and
    kissed
  My forehead, and his arms did round me
    twine,
And held me to his bosom. Still I missed
  That ancient earthly nearness, when we
    shared

One bed, like birds that of no morrow wist ;
  Roamed over our father's farm ; or, later,
    fared
Along the dusty highways of the old clime.
  Backward he drew, and, as if having bared
My soul, stood reading there a little time;
  And in his eyes tears gathered slow, like
    dew
That dims the grass at evening or at prime,
  But makes the stars clear-goldener in the
    blue ;
And on his lips a faint ethereal smile
  Hovered, as hangs the mist of its own hue
Trembling about a purple flower, the while
  Evening grows brown. "Brother! brother!"
    I cried ;
But straight outbursting tears my words be-
    guile,
  And in my bosom all the utterance died.

VII.

A moment more he stood, and softly sighed:—
  "I know thy pain ; but this sorrow is far
Beyond my help ;" at length his voice replied

To my beseeching tears, " Look at yon
    star
Up from the low east half-way—all ablaze ;
    Think'st thou because no cloud between
        doth mar
The liquid glory that from its visage rays,
    Thou therefore knowest that same world
        on high,
Its people and its orders and its ways ? "
    " What meanest thou ? " I said.   " Thou
        know'st that I
Would hold, not thy dear form, but the self-
        thee.
    Thou art not near me.   For thyself I cry."
" Not the less near that nearer I shall be.
    I have a world within thou dost not know;
Would I could make thee know it !   But all
        of me
    Is thine; though thou not yet canst enter so
Into possession, that betwixt us twain
    The frolic homeliness of love should flow
As o'er the brim of childhood's cup again :
    Away the deeper childhood first must wipe
That clouded consciousness which was our
        pain.

When in thy breast the godlike hath grown
    ripe,
And thou, Christ's little one, art ten times
    more
    A child than when we played with drum
      and pipe
About our earthly father's happy door,
    Then—" He ceased not ; his holy utter-
      ance still
Flowing went on like spring from hidden
    store
    Of wasteless waters ; but I wept my fill,
Nor heeded much the comfort of his speech.
    At length he said : "When first I clomb
      the hill—
With earthly words I heavenly things would
    reach—
    Where dwelleth now the man we used to
      call
Father, whose voice—oh memory dear !—did
    teach
    Us in our beds, and straight, as once a stall
A temple, holy grew the sportful room—
    Prone on the ground before him I did fall,
So grand he towered above me like a doom ;
8

But now I look into the well-known face
Fearless, yea, basking blessed in the bloom
  Of his eternal youthfulness and grace."
"But something separates us," yet I cried ;
  " Let light at least begin the dark to chase,
The dark begin to waver and divide,
  And clear the path of vision.   In the old
    time,
When clouds one heart did from the other
    hide,
  A wind would blow between. If one would
    climb,
This foot must rise ere that can go up higher:
  Some big A teach me of the eternal prime."
`He answered then :   "Hearts that to love
    aspire,
  Must learn its mighty harmony ere they can
Falter one perfect note in the great quire.
  Yet thereto am I sent—oh, sent of One
Who makes the dumb for joy break out and
    sing ;
  He opens every door 'twixt man and man;
He to the inner chamber all will bring.".

VIII.

It was enough : hope waked from dreary
    swound,
And hope had ever been enough for me—
To kennel driving grim to-morrow's hound,
    From chains of school and custom setting
    free,
Had urged my life to living.—On we went,
    Across the stars that underlay the sea,
And came to a blown shore of sand and bent.
    Beyond the sand a marshy moor we crossed,
Silent—I, for I pondered what he meant,
    And he, that sacred speech might not be
    lost.
At length we came upon an evil place.
    Trees lay about like a half-buried host,
Each in its desolate pool.   Some fearful race
    Of creatures was not far, for howls and cries
And gurgling hisses came.   With even pace
    Walking, "Fear not," he said, "for this
    way lies
Our journey."   On we went, and soon the
    ground
    Slow from the waste began a gentle rise :

And tender grass, here, there, now all around,
　　Came clouding up, with its fresh homely
　　　tinge
Of softest green cold-flushing every mound ;
　　At length, of lowly shrubs a scattered
　　　fringe.

IX.

And last, a wildered forest, somewhat blind,
　　With a brown shadowless light ; nor, all the
　　　year,
Part once its branches in a blowing wind;
　　So still, its trees, unwithering, appear
To ponder on the past, as men may do
　　That for the future wait without a fear.
I know not if for days many or few
　　Pathless we thrid the wood ; for never sun,
At sylvan-traceried windows peeping through,
　　Mottled with brighter green the mosses dun,
Or meted with moving shadows Time, the
　　　shade.
　　No life was there—not even a spider spun.
At length we came into a sky-roofed glade,
　　An open level, in a circle shut
By solemn trees that stood aside and made
　　Large room and lonely for a little hut,

By grassy sweeps wide-margined from the
    wood.
  'Twas built of saplings old that had been
    cut
When those great trees no larger by them
    stood,
  And, thick with ancient moss, it seemed to
    have grown
Thus from the old brown earth, a covert rude,
  Half-house, half-grave, half-lifted up, half-
    prone.
Up to its door my brother led me. "There
  Is thy low school," he said ; "there be thou
    shown
Thy pictured alphabet. Wake a mind of
    prayer,
  And praying enter." "But wilt thou not
    come,
Brother ?" I said. "No," said he. And I
  —"Where
  Then shall I find thee ? Thou wilt not
    leave me dumb,
And a whole world of thoughts unuttered ?"
  With half-sad smile, and dewy eyes, and
    some

Conflicting motions of his kingly head,
　He pointed to the open-standing door.
I entered : inward, lo, my shadow led !
　　I turned—his countenance shone like
　　　lightning hoar !
But slow he turned from me, and parted slow,
　Like one unwilling, whom I should see no
　　more ;
With voice nor hand, said *Farewell ! I must go,*
　But drew the clinging door hard to the post.
No dry leaves rustled 'neath his going ; no
　Footfalls came back from the departing
　　ghost.
He was no more.　I laid me down and wept,
　Nor dared to follow him—restrained the
　　most
By fear I should not see him if I swept
　Out after him on wings of pleading love.
Close to the wall in hopeless loss I crept.
　　There cool sleep came, God's shadow, from
　　　above.

X.

I woke, with calmness cleansed and sancti-
　fied—

The peace that filled my heart of old,
    when I
Woke in my mother's lap ; for since I died,
    The past lay bare, even to the dreaming shy
That shadowed my yet gathering unborn
    brain.
    And, marvelling, on the floor I saw, close by
My elbow-pillowed head, as if it had lain
    Beside me all the time I dreamless lay,
A little pool of sunlight, which did stain
    The earthen brown with gold ; marvelling,
      I say,
Because across the sea and through the wood
    No sun had shone upon me all the way.
I rose, and through a chink the glade I viewed,
    But all was dull as it before had been,
And sunless every tree-top round it stood,
    With hardly light enough to show it green ;
Yet through the broken roof, serenely glad,
    By a rough hole entered that heavenly
      sheen.
Then I remembered in old years I had
    Seen such a light—where, with dropt eye
      lids gloomed
Upon an earthen floor dark women sad—

In a low barn-like house, where lay en·
tombed
Their sires and children ; only there the door
Was open to the sun, which entering
plumed
With shadowy palms the stones that filled the
floor,
Set up like lidless chests—and so did find
That memory needs no brain, but keeps her
store
In hidden chambers of the eternal mind.
Thence backward ran the rousèd memory
Down the ever-opening vista—back to blind
Anticipations, while my soul did lie
Closed in my mother's ; forward thence
through bright
Spring morns of childhood, gay with hopes
that fly
Bird-like across their doming blue and
white ;
Through passionate summer noons, down to
sad eves
Of autumn rain, and on to wintered night :
Thence up once more to dewy dawn, that
weaves

Saffron and gold—weaves hope with still
content,
And wakes the worship that even wrong be-
reaves
Of half its pain. And round her as she
went,
Hovered a sense as of an odor dear
Whose flower was far—as of a letter sent,
Not yet arrived—a footstep coming near,
But oh! how long delayed the lifting latch!—
As of a waiting sun, ready to peer,
Yet peering not—as of a breathless watch
Over a sleeping beauty—babbling rhyme
About her lips, but no winged word to
catch !
And here I lay—the child of changeful time
Shut in the weary, changeless evermore,
A dull, eternal, fadeless autumn clime !
Was this the dungeon of my sinning sore—
A gentle hell of holiness, foredoomed
For such as I, whose love was yet the core
Of all my being ? The brown shadow gloomed
Persistent, faded, warm. No ripple ran
Across the air, no roaming insect boomed.
"Alas !" I cried, " I am no living man !

Better were darkness and the leave to grope,
  Than light that builds its own drear prison.
  Can
This be the folding of the wings of hope?"

XI.

That instant, through the branches overhead
  Sounds of a going went.   A shadow fell
Prone in the unrippled pool of sunlight fed
  From some far fountain hid in heavenly
   dell.
I looked, and in the low roof's broken place
  A single snowdrop stood—a radiant bell
Of silvery shine, softly subdued by grace
  Of delicate green, that made the white ap-
   pear
Yet whiter.   Blind it bowed its head a space,
  Half-timid—then, as in despite of fear,
It spread its three white rays.   If it had
   swung
  Its pendent bell, and music golden clear—
Division just entrancing sounds among—
  Had flickered down as tender as flakes of
   snow,

It had not shed more influence as it rung
  Than from its look alone did rain and flow.
I knew the flower ; saw too its human ways ;
  Dim saw the secret that had made it grow :
My heart supplied the music's golden phrase.
  Light from the dark and snowdrops from
    the earth—
Life's resurrection out of gross decays—
  The endless round of beauty's yearly birth—
And nations' rise and fall—were in the flower,
  And read themselves in silence. Heavenly
    mirth
Awoke in my sad heart. For one whole hour
  I praised the God of snowdrops. But at
    height
The bliss gave way. Next faith began to
  cower,
  And then the snowdrop vanished from my
    sight.

XII.

Last, I began in unbelief to say :
  " No angel this ! a snowdrop — nothing
    more !
A trifle which God's hands drew forth in play

From the tangled pond of Chaos, dark and
     frore,
And threw on the bank and left blindly to
     breed !
A wilful fancy would have gathered store
Of evanescence from the pretty weed—
     White, pendent — so divine !—conclusion
     lame,
O'erdriven into the shelter of a creed !
     Not out of God, but nothingness, it came :
Colorless, feeble, flying from life's heat,
     It has no honor, hardly shunning shame—"
When—see ! another shadow at my feet !
     Hopeless I lifted now my weary head :
Lo, at my window another heavenly cheat !—
     A primrose fair, from its rough-blanketed bed
Laughing my unbelief to heavenly scorn—
     A sun-child, just awake, no prayer yet said,
Half-rising from the couch where it was born,
     And smiling to the heavens ! I breathed
     again ;
Out of the midnight once more dawned the
     morn !
     And fled the phantom doubt, with all its
     train !

XIII.

I was a child once more, nor measured life,
  Nor thought of what or how much. All my
    soul
With sudden births of lovely things grew rife.
  A daisy at heaven's window ?   Instant roll
Rich lawny fields, with red tips crowding the
    green,
  Across the hollows, over ridge and knoll,
To where the rosy sun goes down serene.
  In at the window peeped a pimpernel ?
I walked in morning scents of thyme and bean;
  Dew-drops on every stalk and bud and bell
Flashed, like a jewel-orchard, many roods ;
  Glowed ruby suns, which emerald suns
    would quell :
Topaz saint-glories, sapphire beatitudes,
  Blazed in the slanting sunshine all around:
Above, the high priest lark, o'er fields and
    woods—
  Rich-hearted with his five eggs on the
    ground—
The sacrifice bore through the veil of light,
  Odor and color offering up in sound.—

Filled heart-full thus with forms of lowly
    might
And shapeful silences of lovely lore,
I sat a child, happy with only sight ;
    And for a time I needed nothing more.

XIV.

Prone to the revelation I did lie—
    Passive as prophet to his dreaming deep,
Or harp Æolian to the breathing sky ;
    And blest as any child whom twilight sleep
Holds half and half lets go. But the new day
    Of higher need up-dawned with sudden
      leap :
" Ah, flowers," I said, " ye are divinely gay !
    But your fair music is too far and fine ;
Ye are full cups, yet reach not to allay
    The drought of those for human love who
      pine,
As harts for water-brooks."   At once a face
    Was looking in my face ; its eyes through
      mine
Were feeding me with tenderness and grace ;
    And by their love I knew my mother's eyes.

And as I gazed there grew in me apace
  A longing grief ; and love did swell and
    rise,
Till weeping I brake out and did bemoan
  My blameful share in bygone tears and
    cries.
" O mother, wilt thou plead for me ? " I groan,
  " I say not, plead with Christ—but plead
    with those
Who, gathered now in peace about his throne,
  Were near me when my heart was full of
    throes,
And longings vain after a flying bliss,
  Which oft the fountain by the threshold
    froze :
They must forgive me, mother. Tell them
    this.
  No more shall swell the love-dividing sigh
Down at their feet I lay my selfishness."
  The face grew passionate at this my cry ;
The gathering tears up to its eyebrims rose ;
  It grew a trembling mist, that did not fly,
But slow dissolved. I wept as one of those
  Who wake outside the garden of the
    dream,

And lo, the droop-winged hours laborious
    close
    Its opal gate with stone and stake and
    beam !

XV.

But glory went that glory more might come.
    Behold a countless multitude—no less !
A host of faces, me besieging, dumb
    In the lone castle of my mournfulness.
Had then my mother given the word I sent,
    And gathered those out of the shining
    press ?
And had these others their love aidance lent
    For full assurance of the pardon prayed ?
Would they concentre love, with sweet intent,
    On my self-love, to blast the evil shade ?
Ah, perfect vision ! pledge of endless hope !
    Oh, army of the Holy Spirit, arrayed
In comfort's panoply ! For words I grope—
    For clouds to catch your radiant dawn, my
    own,
And tell your coming ! From the highest
    cope
    Of blue, down to my windows comes a cone

Of faces and their eyes—O loveliest morn!—
   Bright heads down-bending like the for-
   ward blown,
Heavy with ripeness, golden ears of corn,
   By gentle wind on crowded harvest-field—
All bending to my prison-hut forlorn,
   As if with power of eyes they would have
   healed
My troubled heart—making it like their own,
   In which the bitter fountain had been
   sealed,
And the life-giving water flowed alone !

XVI.

With what I thus beheld, glorified then—
   " God, let me love my fill and pass ! " I
   sighed,
And dead, for love had almost died again.
   " O fathers, brothers, I am yours ! " I cried;
" O mothers, sisters, I am nothing now
   Save as I am yours, and in you sanctified !
O men, O women, of the peaceful brow,
   And infinite abysses in the eyes,
Whence God's ineffable gazes on me ! how
   9

Care ye for me, impassioned and unwise ?
Oh ever draw my heart out after you !
   Ever, O grandeur, thus before me rise,
And I need nothing !—not even for love will
   sue !
   I am no more, and love is all in all.
Henceforth there is, there can be nothing
   new—
   All things are always new." Then, like the
   fall
Of a steep avalanche, my joy fell steep :
   Up in my spirit rose as it were the call
Of an old sorrow from an ancient deep ;
   For when my eyes fixed on the eyes of him
Whom I had loved before I learned to creep—
   God's vicar in his twilight nursery dim,
To gather us about the Saviour's knee—
   I saw a something fill their azure rim
That caught him worlds and years away from
   me ;
   And like a javelin once more through me
   passed
The pang that pierced me walking on the sea.
   " O saints ! " I cried, " must loss be still
   the last ? "

XVII.

When I said this, the cloud of witnesses
  Turned all their faces sideways, and grew
    dim—
So that I saw but half of their sweet bliss,
  And dim as the old moon in the new moon's
    rim.
But as I gazed, a thought, a gleam of light
  On every outline 'gan to glimmer and swim,
Faint as the young moon, threadlike on the
    night,
  Just born of sunbeams trembling on her
    edge.
Was it a smile that broke in luminous white ?
  Or did some dawn begin to drive a wedge
Into the night, and cleave the clinging dark ?
  There was no moon or star, token or pledge
Of light, save that one bordering silvery mark
  Outshaping to my eyes their vanished look.
It swelled and grew.   Suddenly—as a spark
  Of vital touch had found some hidden nook
Where germs of potent harmonies lay prest,
  Whose life outbursting straight the silence
    shook—

Rose in a jubilation calmly blest,
　From that great cone of faces a high song,
Instinct with such harmonical unrest
　That in a flood of weeping—" Lord, how
　　long ? "
I answered it because I could not sing.
　And as they sung, the light more clear and
　　strong
Flamed on their faces, till I scarce could bring
　My eyes the radiance to encounter and
　　bear ;
Light from their eyes, like water from a spring,
Flowed ; on their foreheads reigned their
　　flashing hair ;
And from their lips the great song floated free:
　" O brother ! sister ! *he* comes ! Love is
　　there ! "
Speechless I gazed, thinking—if it were He,
　Then—but the faces moved ! those pre-
　　cious eyes
Were turning on me ! In rushed holy glee,
　And woke me to the dark of lower skies !

XVIII.

As a captive, whom one clank of iron chain

Drags down from dreams of bliss to bitter-
ness,
Stung with its loss, I called the vision vain ;
Yet feeling life grow larger, suffering less,
Dim-eyed, half-raised, I looked into the hush
Of the room—veiled that morning should
not press
Upon the slumber which had stayed the rush
Of ebbing life ; there sat one watching
lone,
And on her brow the dawn's first grayest
flush.
One then was left me of the radiant cone !
Its light on her dear face, though faint and
wan,
Was shining yet—a glimmer to me thrown
From the far coming of the Son of Man !

XIX.

In every forehead now I see a sky
Catching the dawn ; I hear the wintriest
breeze
About me blow the news—the Lord is nigh.
The night is long, dark are the polar seas,

Yet slanting suns ascend the northern hill.
  Round Spring's own steps the oozy waters
    freeze,
But hold them not.   Dreamers yet sleep their
    fill,
  But laborers, light-stung, from their slum-
    ber start.
Faith sees the ripening ears with harvest fill,
  Where but green blades the clinging earth-
    clods part.

XX.

Lord, I have spoken a poor parable—
  In which I would have said thy name alone
Is the one secret lying in Truth's well ;
  Thy voice the hidden charm in music's
    tone ;
Thy face the heart of every flower on earth ;
  Its vision the one hope ; for every moan
Thy love the cure.   O sharer of the birth
  Of little children seated on thy knee !
O human God ! I laugh with sacred mirth
  To think how all the laden must go free ;
For though the vision tarry—in healing ruth
  One morn the eyes that shone in Galilee
Shall dawn upon us, full of grace and truth.

REJOICE.

"REJOICE," said the Sun; "I will make
thee gay
With glory and gladness and holiday;
I am dumb, O man, and I need thy voice."
But man would not rejoice.

"Rejoice in thyself," said he, "O Sun,
For thy daily course is a lordly one;
In thy lofty place, rejoice if thou can;
For me, I am only a man."

"Rejoice," said the Wind; "I am free and
strong;
I will wake in thy heart an ancient song;
Hear the roaring woods, my organ noise!"
But man would not rejoice.

"Rejoice, O Wind, in thy strength," said he,
"For thou fulfillest thy destiny;
Shake the forest, the faint flowers fan:
For me, I am only a man."

"Rejoice," said the Night, "with moon and
star;
The Sun and the Wind are gone afar;

I am here with rest and dreams of choice."
But man would not rejoice.

For he said—" What is rest to me, I pray,
Whose labor brings no gladsome day ?
He only should dream who has hope behind.
Alas for me and my kind ! "

Then a voice that came not from moon or
    star,
From the sun, or the wind roving afar,
Said, " Man, I am with thee—hear my voice."
And man said, " I rejoice."

DO NOT VEX THY VIOLET.

DO not vex thy violet
        Perfume to afford ;
Else no odor thou wilt get
        From its little hoard.

In thy lady's gracious eyes
        Look not thou too long ;
Else from them the glory flies,
        And thou dost her wrong.

UNDERTONES.

WHEN the storm was proudest
 And the wind was loudest,
I heard the hollow caverns drinking down
 below;
 When the stars were bright
 And the ground was white,
I heard the grasses springing underneath the
 snow.

 Many voices spake—
 The river to the lake,
The iron-ribbed sky was talking to the sea ;
 And every starry spark
 Made music with the dark
And said how bright and beautiful everything
 must be.

 When the sun was setting,
 All the clouds were getting
Beautiful and silvery in the rising moon ;
 Beneath the leafless trees
 Wrangling in the breeze,
I could hardly see them for the leaves of
 June.

When the day had ended
And the night descended,
I heard the sound of streams that I heard not
　　through the day;
And every peak afar
Was ready for a star,
And they climbed and rolled around till the
　　morning gray.

Then slumber soft and holy
Came down upon me slowly;
And I went I know not whither and I lived I
　　know not how;
My glory had been banished,
For when I woke it vanished—
But I waited on its coming and I am waiting
　　now.

———

WILD FLOWERS.

HOW is it with you, children all,
　　When human children on you fall,
Gather you in eager haste,
Forget your beauty in their waste,

Fill and fill their full-filled hands?
Goeth a tearing through your breast,
A fainting, melting of your bands?
Do you know
When the spoilers near you come
By a shuddering in your gloom?
For blind and deaf we think you are,
Hearing, seeing, near nor far :
Is it so?
Is it only ye are dumb?
You alive at least I think,
Trembling almost on the brink
Of our lonely consciousness :
If it be so,
Take this comfort for your woe,
For the breaking of your rest,
For the tearing in your breast,
For the blotting of your sun,
For the death too soon begun,
For all else beyond redress,
For the thing ye cannot be—
That the children's wonder-springs
Bubble high at sight of you,
Lovely, lowly, common things—
More believing than they see,

When ye float into their view;
That ye, bravely creeping out,
Smile away our manhood's doubt,
And our childhood's faith renew;
And that we, with old age nigh,
Seeing you alive and well
Out of winter's crucible—
You who from the grave have crept,
Telling us ye only slept—
Think we die not, though we die.
Thus ye die not, though ye die—
Only yield your being up,
Like a nectar-holding cup:
Deaf, ye give to them that hear,
With a greatness lovely-dear,
Blind, ye give to them that see—
Poor, but bounteous royally.
Lowly servants to the higher,
Burning upwards in the fire
Of nature's endless sacrifice,
Thus in life's ascent ye rise;
Thus you leave the earth behind,
And pass into the human mind,
Pass with it up into God,
Whence ye came down through the clod—

Pass, and find yourselves at home
Where but life can go and come ;
Where all life is in its nest,
At holy one with awful Best.

FULFILMENT.

I ENTERED Nature's church, a shimmer-
ing vault
Of boughs, and clouded leaves—filmy and
pale
Betwixt me and the sun ; low at my feet
Their shadows looked more solid than them-
selves,
And lay like tombstones o'er the vanished
flowers.
Silent the plane, except for broken songs
Of some Memnonian, glory-stricken birds
That burst into a carol and were still ;
And moveless but that golden beetles crept,
Green goblins, in the roots ; and squirrel
things
Ran, wild as cherubs, through the tracery ;
And here and yonder a flaky butterfly
Was doubting in the air, scarlet and blue.

But 'twixt my heart and summer's perfect
     grace,
Drove a dividing wedge ;—and far away
It seemed, like voice heard loud yet far away
By one who, waking half, soon sleeps outright.
—Where was the snowdrop ? where the flower
     of hope ?
In me the spring was throbbing—and around
I saw the resting, odor-breathing summer !
My heart heaved swelling like a prisoned bud,
And summer crushed it with its weight of
     light.

Winter is full of stings and sharp reproofs,
Lovely and needful, but like cold sister's
     words ;
And summer is too complete for growing
     hearts ;
Too idle its noons, too arrowy its morns,
Too full of slumberous dreams its dusky eves.
We need a broken season, and a land
Whose shadows ever point from here away ;
A scheme of cones abrupt, and shattered
     spheres,
And circles cut to widen evermore.

To us, a flower of winter-harassed spring,
Crocus, or primrose, or anemone,
Is lovely as was never rosiest rose ;
A heath-bell on a waste lonely and dry
Says more than lily stately in breathing white ;
A window fair through vaulted roof of rain,
Lets in a light that comes from farther away,
And, sinking deeper, spreads a finer joy,
Than cloudless noon-tide splendorous o'er
    the world.
Man seeks a better home than Paradise ;
Therefore high hope is more than deepest joy;
The first meek daisy on a wind-swept lea,
Dearer than Eden-groves with rivers four.

    Yet if my heart were pure, perhaps the rose
Were but the primrose of a higher spring ;
The sunflower but a daisy of the prime
That leads high summer in for full-blown
    hearts.

EARTH'S RESTLESSNESS.

COMES there, O Earth, no breathing-time
    for thee ?
No pause upon thy many-chequered lands?
Now resting on my bed with listless hands

I mourn thee resting not.   Continually
Hear I the plashing borders of the sea
Answer each other from the rocks and sands ;
Troop all the rivers seaward.   Nothing stands,
But with strange noises hasteth terribly.
Loam-eared hyenas go a moaning by,
Howls to each other all the bloody crew
Of Afric's tigers.   But, O man, from you
Comes this perpetual sound more loud and
   high
Than aught that vexes air.   I hear the cry
Of infant generations rising too.

THE FAILING TRACK.

WHERE went the feet that hitherto
      have come ?
   Here yawns no gulf to quench the flowing
      Past.
With lengthening pauses broke, the path
      grows dumb ;
   The grass floats in ; the gazer stands aghast.

Tremble not, maiden.   Let the footprints die.
   No trodden way leads up the skylark's
      notes ;

The mighty-throated, when he mounts the
  sky,
  Over some lowly landmark sings and floats.

Be of good cheer. Paths vanish from the
  wave
  Where thousand ships have torn their tracks
    of gray;
But ships undaunted still the desert brave :
  In each a magic finger points the way.

No finger finely touched, no eye of lark,
  Hast thou to guide thy steps where foot-
    prints fail ?
Ah, then, 'twere well to turn before the dark,
  Nor dream to find thy dreams in yonder
    vale !

The backward path one hour is plain to see—
  Hapless wert thou, if that were lost behind!
Back to the prayer beside thy mother's knee—
  Back to the question and the childlike mind!

Then start afresh—but toward some noble
  end,
    10

Some goal o'er which hangs a known star
    all night ;
So shalt thou need no footprints to befriend :
    Child-heart and shining star will guide thee
    right.

THE JOURNEY.

I.

HARK, the rain is on my roof !
    Every murmur, through the dark,
Stings me with a dull reproof,
    Like a half-extinguished spark.
It is I ! but how come here—
    Wide awake and wide alone—
Caught within a net of fear—
    All my dreams dreamed out and gone ?

I will rise ; I will go forth.
    Better face the hideous night,
Better dare the harmful north,
    Than be mastered with affright !
Black wind rushing—every blast
    Sown with arrowy points of rain !

Time and place are gone and past—
  I am here, and so is pain!

Dead in dreams the gloomy street!
  I will out on open roads.
Eager grow my aimless feet—
  Onward, onward something goads.
I will take the mountain path,
  Beard the storm within its den;
Know the worst of this dim wrath
  Harassing the souls of men.

Chasm 'neath chasm! rock piled on rock!
  Roots, and crumbling earth, and stones!
Hark, the torrent's thundering shock!
  Hark, the swaying pine tree's groans!
Ah! I faint, I fall, I die—
  Sink to nothingness away!
Lo, a streak upon the sky!—
  Lo, the opening eye of day!

II.

Mountain summits lift their snows
  O'er a valley green and low;
And a winding pathway goes
  Guided by the river's flow:

And a music rises ever,
  As of peace and low content,
From the pebble-paven river,
  Like an odor, upward sent.

And the sound of ancient harms
  Moans behind, the hills among,
Like the humming of the swarms
  That unseen the forest throng.
Now I meet the shining rain
  From a cloud with sunny weft ;
Now against the wind I strain,
  Sudden burst from mountain cleft.

Now a sky that hath a moon,
  Staining all the cloudy white
With a faded rainbow—soon
  Lost in deeps of heavenly night !
Now a morning clear and soft,
  Amber on the purple hills ;
Warm blue day of summer, oft
  Cooled by wandering windy rills !

Joy to travel thus along,
  With the universe around !

Every creature of the throng,
　Every sight and scent and sound
Homeward speeds with beauty laden,
　Beelike, to its hive, my soul !
Mine the eye the stars are made in !
　Mine the heart of Nature's whole !

III.

Hills retreat on either hand,
　Sinking slowly to the plain ;
Solemn through the outspread land
　Rolls the river to the main.
As the twilight grows the night,
　Something through the dusky air
Doubtful glimmers, faintly white,
　But I know not what nor where.

Is it but a chalky ridge,
　Bared of sod, like tree of bark ?
Or a river-spanning bridge,
　Miles away into the dark ?
Or the foremost leaping waves
　Of the everlasting sea,
Where the Undivided laves
　Time with its eternity ?

Is it but an eye-made sight—
  In my brain a fancied gleam ?
Or a faint aurora-light
  From the sun's tired smoking team ?
Known shall be the thing unknown,
  When the morning climbs the sky ;
In the darkness it is gone,
  Yet with every step draws nigh.

Onward, onward through the night !
  Matters it I cannot see ?
I am moving in a might
  Dwelling in the dark and me.
End or way I cannot lose—
  Grudge to rest, or fear to roam ;
All is well with wanderer whose
  Heart is travelling hourly home.

IV.

Joy ! oh joy ! the dawning sea
  Answers to the dawning sky ;
Foretaste of the coming glee
  When the sun will lord it high.
See the swelling radiance grow
  To a dazzling glory-might !

Thoughtful shadows gently go
   'Twixt the wave tops wild with light !

Hear the smiting billows clang !
   See the falling billows lean
Half a watery vault, and hang
   Gleaming with translucent green—
Then in thousand fleeces lie,
   Thundering light upon the strand ! —
Vague it reached my doubting eye
   Through the dusk, across the land.

See, a boat ! Out, out we dance !
   Fierce wind swoops my fluttering sail !
What a terrible expanse—
   Tumbling hill and heaving dale !
Restless, helpless, lost I float—
   Captive to the lawless free !
And my prison is my boat—
   Oh, for petrel wings to flee !

Look below : each watery whirl
   Cast in beauty's living mould !
Look above : each feathery curl
   Dropping crimson, dropping gold !—

Oh, I tremble in the gush
Of an everlasting youth !
Love and fear together rush :
I am free,—in God, the truth !

DREAM SONG.

A SPLENDOR of dreaming o'erflowed
    her ;
A glory that deepened and grew ;
A song of color and odor
    That thrilled her through and through !
'Twas a dream of too much gladness
    Ever to see the light ;
They are only dreams of sadness
    That weary out the night.

Slow darkness began to rifle
    The nest of the sunset fair ;
Dank vapor began to stifle
    The scents that enriched the air.
And the flowers paled fast and faster,
    And crumbled leaf and crown,
Till they looked like the stainèd plaster
    Of a cornice fallen down.

DREAM SONG. 153

And the change crept nigher and nigher,
    And inward and nearer stole,
Till the flameless but blasting fire
    Entered and withered her soul.—
But the fiend had only flouted
    Her visions of the night ;
Up came the morn and routed
    The darksome things with light.

Wide awake I have often been in it—
    The dream that all is none ;
It will come in the gladdest minute
    And wither the very sun.
Two moments of sad commotion,
    One more of doubt's palsied rule—
And the great wave-pulsing ocean
    Is only a gathered pool ;

And a flower is a spot of painting,
    A lifeless, loveless hue :
Though your heart be sick to fainting,
    It says not a word to you ;
And a bird knows nothing of gladness—
    Is only a song-machine ;
A man is a reasoning madness,
    And a woman a pictured queen.

Then fiercely we dig the fountain—
    Oh ! whence do the waters rise ?
Then panting we climb the mountain—
    Oh ! are there indeed blue skies ?
And we dig till the soul is weary,
    Nor find the waters out ;
And we climb till all is dreary,
    And still the sky is a doubt.

Search not the roots of the fountain,
    But drink the water bright ;
Gaze far above the mountain—
    The sky may speak in light.
But if yet thou see no beauty—
    If widowed thy heart yet cries—
With thy hands go and do thy duty,
    And thy work will clear thine eyes.

———

A BLIGHTING fog uprises with the days,
    False, cold, dull, leaden, gray. It
        clings about
The present, far dragging like a robe ; but
    ever
Forsakes the past, and lets its hues shine out :

On past and future pours the light of heaven.
The Commonplace is of the present mind.
The lovely is the True.   The Beautiful
Is what God made.   Men from whose narrow
  bosoms
The great child-heart has withered, backward
  look
To their first love, and laugh, and call it folly,
A mere delusion to which youth is subject,
As childhood to diseases. They know better ;
And proud of their denying, tell the youth,
On whom the wonder of his being shines,
That will be over with him by and by :
" I was so when a boy—look at me now ! "
Youth, be not one of them, but love thy love.
So with all worship of the high and good,
And pure and beautiful. These men are wiser !
Their god, Experience, but their own decay ;
Their wisdom but the gray hairs gathered on
  them.
Yea, some will mourn and sing about their
  loss,
And for the sake of sweet sounds cherish it,
Nor yet believe that it was more than seem-
  ing.

But he in whom the child's heart hath not
    died,
Hath grown a man's heart, loveth yet the
    Past ;
Believes in all its beauty ; knows the hours
Will melt the mist ; and though this very day
Casts but a dull stone on Time's heaped-up
    cairn,
A morning light will break one morn and
    draw
The hidden glories of a thousand hues
Out from its crystal-depths and ruby-spots
And sapphire-veins, unseen, unknown, before.
Far in the future lies his refuge.   Time
Is God's, and all his miracles are his ;
And in the Future he overtakes the Past,
Which was a prophecy of times to come :
There lie great flashing stars, the same that
    shone
In childhood's laughing heaven ; there lies
    the wonder
In which the sun went down and moon arose;
The joy with which the meadows opened out
Their daisies to the warming sun of spring ;
Yea, all the inward glory, ere cold fear

Froze, or doubt shook the mirror of his soul.
To reach it, he must climb the present slope
Of this day's duty—here he would not rest.
But all the time the glory is at hand,
Urging and guiding—only o'er its face
Hangs ever, pledge and screen, the bridal
    veil :
He knows the beauty radiant underneath ;
He knows that God who is the living God,
The God of living things, not of the dying,
Would never give his child, for God-born
    love,
A cloud-made phantom, fading in the sun.
Faith vanishes in sight ; the cloudy veil
Will melt away, destroyed of inward light.
          —From *Within and Without.*

THE FATHER'S HYMN FOR THE MOTHER TO SING.

MY child is lying on my knees ;
    The signs of heaven she reads ;
My face is all the heaven she sees,
    Is all the heaven she needs.

And she is well, yea, bathed in bliss,
  If heaven is in my face—
Behind it all is tenderness,
  And truthfulness and grace.

I mean her well so earnestly,
  Unchanged in changing mood ;
My life would go without a sigh
  To bring her something good.

I also am a child, and I
  Am ignorant and weak ;
I gaze upon the starry sky,
  And then I must not speak ;

For all behind the starry sky,
  Behind the world so broad,
Behind men's hearts and souls doth lie
  The Infinite of God.

If true to her, though troubled sore,
  I cannot choose but be ;
Thou, who art peace for evermore,
  Art very true to me.

If I am low and sinful, bring
  More love where need is rife ;

Thou knowest what an awful thing
It is to be a life.

Hast thou not wisdom to enwrap
My waywardness about,
In doubting safety on the lap
Of Love that knows no doubt ?

Lo ! Lord, I sit in thy wide space,
My child upon my knee ;
She looketh up into my face,
And I look up to thee.

THE STRENGTH OF PATIENCE.

IF thou art tempted by a thought of ill,
  Crave not too soon for victory, nor deem
·Thou art a coward if thy safety seem
To spring too little from a righteous will :
For there is nightmare on thee, nor until
Thy soul hath caught the morning's early
    gleam
Seek thou to analyze the monstrous dream
By painful introversion ; rather fill

Thine eye with forms thou knowest to be
  truth ;
But see thou cherish higher hope than this—
A hope hereafter that thou shalt be fit
Calm-eyed to face distortion, and to sit
Transparent among other forms of youth
Who own no impulse save to God and bliss.

————

LIGHT.

WE lay us down in sorrow,
      Wrapt in the old mantle of our
  mother Night ;
In vexing dreams we strive until the morrow ;
Grief lifts our eyelids up—and lo, the light !
The sunlight on the wall ! And visions rise
Of shining leaves that make sweet melodies ;
Of wind-borne waves with thee upon their
  crests ;
Of rippled sands on which thou rainest down;
Of quiet lakes that smooth for thee their
  breasts ;
Of clouds that show thy glory as their own ;
O joy ! O joy ! the visions are gone by !
Light, gladness, motion, are reality !

Thou art the god of earth.   The skylark
    springs
Far up to catch thy glory on his wings ;
And thou dost bless him first that highest
    soars.
The bee comes forth to see thee ; and the
    flowers
Worship thee all day long, and through the
    skies
Follow thy journey with their earnest eyes.
River of life, thou pourest on the woods,
And on thy waves float out the wakening buds.
The trees lean towards thee, and, in loving
    pain,
Keep turning still to see thee yet again.
And nothing in thy eyes is mean or low :
Where'er thou art, on every side,
All things are glorified ;
And where thou canst not come, there thou
    dost throw
Beautiful shadows, made out of the dark,
That else were shapeless ; now it bears thy
    mark.

     *   *   *   *   *   *

When the firstborn affections—

11

Those wingèd seekers of the world within,
That search about in all directions,
Some bright thing for themselves to win—
Through pathless forests, gathering fogs,
Through stony plains, treacherous bogs,
Long, long, have followed faces fair,
Fair soulless faces which have vanished into
　　air ;
And darkness is around them and above,
Desolate, with naught to love ;
And through the gloom on every side,
Strange dismal forms are dim descried ;
And the air is as the breath
From the lips of void-eyed Death ;
And the knees are bowed in prayer
To the stronger than despair ;
Then the ever-lifted cry,
Give us light, or we shall die,
Cometh to the Father's ears,
And he hearkens, and he hears;
And slow, as if some sun would glimmer
　　forth
From sunless winter of the north,
They, hardly trusting happy eyes,
Discern a dawning in the skies :

'Tis Truth awaking in the soul ;
Thy Righteousness to make them whole.
—What shall men, this Truth adoring,
Gladness-giving, youth-restoring,
Call it but eternal Light ?—
'Tis the morning, 'twas the night.
Even a misty hope that lies on
Our dim future's far horizon,
We call a fresh aurora, sent
Up the spirit's firmament,
Telling, through the vapors dun,
Of the coming, coming sun.

All things most excellent
Are likened unto thee, excellent thing !
Yea, he who from the Father forth was sent,
Came like a lamp to bring,
Across the winds and wastes of night,
The everlasting light ;
The Word of God, the telling of his thought;
The Light of God, the making-visible ;
The far-transcending glory brought
In human form with man to dwell ;
The dazzling gone ; the power not less
To show, irradiate, and bless :

The gathering of the primal rays divine,
Informing chaos, to a pure sunshine !

Gentle winds through forests calling !
Bright birds through the thick leaves glancing!
Solemn waves on sea-shores falling !
White sails on blue waters dancing !
Mountain streams glad music giving !
Children in the clear pool laving !
Yellow corn and green grass waving !
Long-haired, bright-eyed maidens living !
Light, O Radiant ! it is thou !
And we know our Father now.

Forming ever without form ;
Showing, but thyself unseen ;
Pouring stillness on the storm ;
Making life where death had been !
Light, if He did draw thee in,
Death and Chaos soon were out,
Weltering o'er the slimy sea,
Riding on the whirlwind's rout,
In unmaking energy !
Thou art round us, God within,
Fighting darkness, slaying sin.

Father of Lights, high-lost, unspeakable,
On whom no changing shadow ever fell !
Thy light we know not, are content to see ;
And shall we doubt because we know not
    thee ?
Or, when thy wisdom cannot be expressed,
Fear lest dark vapors brood within thy breast?
It shall not be ;
Our hearts awake and speak aloud for thee.
The very shadows on our souls that lie,
Good witness to the light supernal bear ;
The something 'twixt us and the sky
Could cast no shadow if light were not there.
If children tremble in the night,
It is because their God is light.
The shining of the common day
Is mystery still, howe'er it ebb and flow ;
Behind the seeing orb, the secret lies :
Thy living light's eternal play,
Its motions, whence or whither, who shall
    know ?—
Behind the life itself, its fountains rise.

Enlighten me, O Light ! why art thou such ?
Why art thou awful to our eyes, and sweet ? .

Cherished as love, and slaying with a touch ?
Why in thee do the known and the unknown
    meet ?
Why swift and tender, strong and delicate ?
Simple as truth, yet manifold in might ?
Why does one love thee, and another hate ?
Why cleave my words to the portals of my
    speech,
When I a goodly matter would indite ?
Why fly my thoughts themselves beyond my
    reach ?
—In vain to follow thee, I thee beseech,
For God is light.

WIN' THAT BLAWS THE SIMMER PLAID.

WIN' that blaws the simmer plaid,
    Ower the hie hill's shouthers laid,
Green wi' gerse, and reid wi' heather,
Welcome wi' yer soul-like weather !
Mony a win' there has been sent
Oot 'aneth the firmament ;
Ilka ane its story has :
Ilka ane began an' was ;

Ilka ane fell quaiet an' mute
Whan its angel wark was oot.
First gaed ane oot ower the mirk,
Whan the maker gan to work ;
Ower it gaed and ower the sea,
An' the warl' begun to be.
Mony ane has come an' gane
Sin' the time there was but ane :
Ane was great an' strong, an' rent
Rocks an' mountains as it went
Afore the Lord, his trumpeter,
Waukin' up the prophet's ear ;
Ane was like a steppin' soun'
I' the mulberry taps abune ;
Them the Lord's ain steps did swing,
Walkin' on afore his king ;
Ane lay doon like scoldit pup
At his feet an' gatna up,
Whan the word the maistre spak
Drave the wull-cat billows back ;
Ane gaed frae his lips, an' dang
To the earth the sodger thrang ;
Ane comes frae his hert to mine,
Ilka day, to mak it fine.
Breath o' God, eh ! come an' blaw

Frae my hert ilk fog awa';
Wauk me up, an' mak me strang,
Fill my hert wi' mony a sang.
Frae my lips again to stert,
Fillin' sails o' mony a hert,
Blawin' them ower seas dividin'
To the only place to bide in.

O LASSIE AYONT THE HILL!

O LASSIE ayont the hill,
   Come ower the tap o' the hill,
Come ower the tap wi' the breeze o' the hill,
   For I want ye sair the nicht.
   I'm needin' ye sair the nicht,
For I'm tired and sick o' mysel'.
   A body's sel' 's the sairest weicht:
O lassie, come ower the hill !

Gin a body cud be a thocht o' grace,
   And no a sel' ava !
I'm sick o' my heid and my han's and my
    face,
   O' my thochts and mysel' an' a'.
   I'm sick o' the warl' an' a' ;
The win' gangs by wi' a hiss ;

Throu my stairin' een the sunbeams fa',
But my weary hert they miss.
   O lassie ayont the hill !
   Come ower the tap o' the hill,
   Come ower the tap wi' the breeze o' the
      hill;
   Bidena ayont the hill.

For gin I but saw yer bonnie heid,
   And the sunlicht o' yer hair,
The ghaist o' mysel' wad fa' doun deid,
   I wad be mysel' nae mair.
   I wad be mysel' nae mair,
Filled o' the sole remeid—
   Slain by arrows o' licht frae yer hair,
Killed by yer body and heid.
   O lassie ayont the hill ! etc.

Mysel' micht wauk up at the saft fitfa'
   O my bonnie depairtin' dame ;
But gin she lo'ed me ever sae sma',
   I micht bide it—the weary same ;
   Noo, sick o' my body and name,
When it lifts its upsettin' heid,

I turn frae the cla'es that cover my frame,
As gin they war roun' the deid.
O lassie ayont the hill ! etc.

But gin ye lo'ed me as I lo'e you,
I wad ring my ain deid knell ;
The spectre wad melt, shot through and
through
Wi' the shine o' yer sunny sel'.—
By the shine o' yer sunny sel',
By the licht aneth yer broo,
I wad dee to mysel', ring my ain deid-
bell,
And live forever in you.

O lassie ayont the hill !
Come ower the tap o' the hill,
Come ower the tap wi' the breeze o' the hill,
For I want ye sair the nicht.
I'm needin' ye sair the nicht,
For I'm tired and sick o' mysel'.
A body's sel' 's the sairest weicht :
O lassie, come ower the hill !

THE BONNY, BONNY DELL.

OH ! the bonny, bonny dell, whaur the
yorlin sings,
Wi' 'a clip o' the sunshine atween his wings ;
Whaur the birks are a' straikit wi' fair mune-
licht,
And the brume hings its lamps by day and by
nicht ;
Whaur the burnie comes trottin' ower shingle
and stane,
Liltin' bonny havers til 'tsel' alane ;
And the sliddery troot wi' ae soop o' its tail
Is ahint the green weed's dark swingin' veil !
Oh ! the bonny, bonny dell, whaur I sang as
I saw
The yorlin, the brume, and the burnie, an' a' !
Oh ! the bonny, bonny dell, whaur the prim-
roses wonn,
Luikin' oot o' their leaves like wee sons o' the
sun ;
Whaur the wild roses hing like flickers o'
flame,
And fa' at the touch wi' a dainty shame ;

Whaur the bee swings ower the white-clovery
  sod,
And the butterfly flits like a stray thoucht o'
  God ;
Whaur, like arrow shot frae life's unseen bow,
The dragon-fly burns the sunlicht throu !
Oh ! the bonny, bonny dell, whaur I sang to
  see
The rose and the primrose, the draigon and
  bee !

Oh ! the bonny, bonny dell, whaur the mune
  luiks doon,
As gin she war hearin' a soughless tune,
Whan the flooers an' the birdies are a' asleep,
And the verra burnie gangs creepy-creep ;
Whaur the corn-craik craiks,i' the lang-heidit
  rye,
And the night is the safter for his rouch cry ;
Whaur the win' wad fain lay doon on the
  slope,
And the gloamin' waukens the high-reachin'
  · hope !
Oh ! the bonny, bonny dell, whaur, silent, I
  felt

The mune and the darkness baith into me
  melt !

Oh ! the bonny, bonny dell, whaur the sun
  luiks in,
Sayin', Here awa', there awa', haud awa', sin;
Sayin', Darkness and sorrow a' work for the
  licht,
And the will o' God was the hert o' the nicht;
Whaur the laverock hings hie, on his ain sang
  borne,
Wi' bird-shout and tirralee hailin' the morn ;
Whaur my hert ran ower wi' the lusome bliss,
That, come mirk or come winter, nocht gaed
  amiss !
Oh ! the bonny, bonny dell, whaur the sun
  luikit in,
Sayin', Here awa' there awa', haud awa', sin!

Oh ! the bonny, bonny dell, whaur aft I wad
  lie,
Wi' Jeanie aside me, sae sweet and sae shy !
Whaur the starry gowans wi' rose-dippit tips,
War as white as her cheek and as reid as her
  lips ;

Whaur she spread her gowd hert till she saw
  that I saw,
Syne fauldit it up and gae me it a';
Whaur o' sunlicht and munelicht she was the
  queen,
For baith war but middlin' withoot my Jean!
Oh ! the bonny, bonny dell, whaur aft I wad
  lie,
Wi' Jeanie aside me, sae sweet and sae shy !

Oh! the bonny, bonny dell, whaur the kirkyard
  lies,
A' day an' a' nicht, luikin' up to the skies ;
Whaur the sheep wauken up i' the simmer
  nicht,
Tak a bite, and lie doon, an' await the licht;
Whaur the psalms roll ower the grassy heaps;
Whaur the wind comes and moans, and the
  rain comes and weeps ;
Whaur my Jeanie's no lyin' in a' the lair,
For she's up an' awa' up the angel's stair !
Oh! the bonny, bonny dell, whaur the kirkyard
  lies,
Whaur the stairs luik doon, and the nicht-
  wind sighs !

A SANG O' ZION.

ANE by ane they gang awa';
   The gaitherer gaithers grit and sma':
Ane by ane makes ane an' a'.

Aye when ane sets doon the cup,
Ane ahint maun tak it up ;
Yet thegither they will sup.

Golden-heidit, ripe, and strang,
Shorn will be the hairst or lang :
Syne begins a better sang.

HOPE DEFERRED.

SUMMER is come again. The sun is
   bright,
And the soft wind is breathing. Airy joy
Is sparkling in thine eyes, and in their light
My soul is shining. Come; our day's employ
Shall be to revel in unlikely things,
In gayest hopes, fondest imaginings,

And make-believes of bliss.   Come, we will
　　talk
Of waning moons, low winds, and a dim sea,
Till this fair summer, deepening as we walk,
Has grown a paradise for you and me.
But ah, those leaves !—it was not summer's
　　mouth
Breathed such a gold upon them.   And look
　　there—
That beech how red !   See, through its boughs
　　half bare,
How low the sun lies in the mid-day south !—
'Tis but a wandering memory that hath shone
Back from the summer mourning to be gone.
See, see the dead leaves falling !   Hear thy
　　heart,
Which, changing ever as seasons come and
　　go,
Takes in the changing world its mournful
　　part,
Return a sigh, an echo sad and low
To the faint, half inaudible sound
With which the leaf goes whispering to the
　　ground !
O love, the winter lieth at the door—

Behind the winter, age and something more.
  Come round me, dear hearts. All of us
    will hold
Each one encompassed : we are growing old;
And if we be not as a ring enchanted
Around each heart, with love to keep it gay,
The young, who claim the joy that haunted
Our visions once, will push us far away
Into the desolate regions, dim and gray,
Where the sea moans, and hath no other cry,
The cloud is mist, and hath no rain of tears,
The past sinks swallowed in a pit of years,
And hopes and joys both careless pass us by;
But if all each do keep,
The rising tide of youth will sweep
Around us with its laughter-joyous waves,
As ocean fair some palmy island laves,
To loneliness heaved slow from out the deep;
And our lost youth keep hovering like the
    breath
Round one that sleeps, and sleepeth not to
    death.
  Bound thus together, on to parted graves,
The sundered doors into one palace home,
Stumbling through age's thickets we will go,

Faltering but faithful—willing to lie low,
Willing to part, not willing to deny
The lovely past, where all the futures lie.
   Oh ! if thou be—called of the living lord,
Not of the dead—lo ! by that self-same word
Thou art not lord of age, but lord of youth ;
Because there is no age, in sooth,
Beyond its passing shows :
A mist o'er life's dimmed lantern grows;
But when the glass is broken, lo, the light
That knows not youth nor age,
That fears no darkness nor the rage
Of windy tempests—burning still more bright
Than when glad youth was all about,
And summer winds were out !

SPRING SONG.

DAYS of old,
      Ye are not dead, though
gone from me ;
      Ye are not cold,
But like summer birds fled o'er some sea.

The sun brings back the swallows fast
    O'er the sea:
When he cometh at the last,
    The days of old come back to me.

—————

THE HOLY MIDNIGHT.

AH, holy midnight of the soul,
    When stars alone are high;
When winds are resting at their goal,
    And sea-waves only sigh !

Ambition faints from out the will ;
    Asleep sad longing lies ;
All hope of good, all fear of ill,
    All need of action dies ;

Because God is; and claims the life
    He kindled in thy brain ;
And thou in him, rapt far from strife,
    Diest and liv'st again.

REST.   .

THERE is a rest that deeper grows
    In midst of pain and strife ;
A mighty, conscious, willed repose,
    The death of deepest life.
To have and hold the precious prize
    No need of jealous bars ;
But windows open to the skies,
    And skill to read the stars.

Who dwelleth in that secret place,
    Where tumult enters not,
Is never cold with terror base,
    Never with anger hot.
For if an evil host should dare
    His very heart invest,
God is his deeper heart, and there
    He enters into rest.

When mighty sea-winds madly blow,
    And tear the scattered waves,
Peaceful as summer woods, below
    Lie darkling ocean caves :

The wind of words may toss my heart,
　But what is that to me !
'Tis but a surface storm—thou art
　My deep, still resting sea.

———

PARTING.

THOU goest thine, and I go mine—
　Many ways we wend ;
Many days, and many ways,
　Ending in one end.

Many a wrong, and its curing song ;
　Many a road, and many an inn ;
Room to roam, but only one home
　For all the world to win.

POEMS FOR CHILDREN.

THE WONDER.

BABY, with her pretty prate,
    Molten, half articulate,
Full of hints, suggestions, catches,
Broken verse, and music snatches,
Like an angel gone astray,
Must be taught the homeward way;
Plant of heaven, she, rooted lowly,
Must put forth a blossom holy,
Must, with culture high and steady,
Slow unfold a gracious lady;
We must keep her full of wonder
At the daisy at the thunder,
At the moon and stars and sea,
At the butterfly and bee;
Never her and childhood part,
Change the brain, but keep the heart.

So, from lips and hands and looks,
She must learn to honor books,
Yet must learn that mere *appearing*
Gives no title to revering ;
That a pump is not a well,
Nor a priest an oracle :
Sight convincing to her mind,
I will separate kind from kind,
And those books, though honored by her,
Gently lay upon the fire ;
Sacred form even shall not hinder
Their consumption to a cinder.

Would you see the slight immortal,
One short pace within our portal ?
I will fetch her.—See how white !
Solemn pure—a light in light !
Gleaming frock and lily-skin
White as whitest ermelin
Washed in palest, thinnest rose !
Like a thought of God she goes,
Wandering ever in the dance
Of her own sweet radiance :
Books and music far asunder—
Of all wonders, she's the wonder !

LITTLE WHITE LILY.

L ITTLE white Lily,
   Sat by a stone,
Drooping and waiting
   Till the sun shone.
Little white Lily
   Sunshine has fed ;
Little white Lily
   Is lifting her head.

Little white Lily
   Said, " It is good :
Little white Lily's
   Clothing and food !
Little white Lily
   Drest like a bride !
Shining with whiteness
   And crownèd beside ! "

Little white Lily
   Droopeth in pain,
Waiting and waiting
   For the wet rain.

Little white Lily
  Holdeth her cup :
Rain is fast falling
  And filling it up.

Little white Lily
  Said, " Good again,
When I am thirsty
  To have nice rain !
Now I am stronger,
  Now I am cool ;
Heat cannot burn me,
  My veins are so full ! "

Little white Lily
  Smells very sweet :
On her head sunshine,
  Rain at her feet.
"Thanks to the sunshine !
  Thanks to the rain !
Little white Lily
  Is happy again ! "

THE WAKEFUL SLEEPER.

WHEN things are holding wonted pace
    In wonted paths, without a trace
Or hint of neighboring wonder,
Sometimes, from other realms, a tone,
A scent, a vision, swift, alone,
    Breaks common life asunder.

Howe'er it comes, whate'er its door,
It makes you ponder something more—
    Unseen with seen things linking.
To neighbors met one festive night,
Was given a quaint and lovely sight,
    That set some of them thinking.

They stand, in music's fetters bound,
By a clear brook of warbled sound—
    A canzonet of Haydn—
When the door slowly comes ajar—
A little further—just as far
    As shows a tiny maiden.

Softly she enters, her pink toes
Daintily peeping, as she goes,
    Her long nightgown from under.

The varied mien, the questioning look
Were worth a picture ; but she took
    No notice of their wonder.

They made a path, and she went through :
She had her little chair in view,
    Close by the chimney-corner.
She turned—sat down before them all,
Stately as princess at a ball,
    And silent as a mourner.

Then looking closer yet, they spy
What mazedness hid from every eye,
    As ghost-like she came creeping ;
They see that though sweet little Rose
Her settled way unerring goes,
    The child is plainly sleeping.

" Play on, sing on," the mother said ;
" Oft music draws her from her bed."—
    Dumb Echo, she sat listening.
Over her face the sweet concent
Like winds o'er placid waters went ;
    Her cheeks like eyes were glistening.

Her hands tight-clasped her bent knees
  hold ;
Like long grass drooping on the wold,
  Her sightless head is bending ;
She sits all ears, and drinks her fill ;
Then rising goes, sedate and still,
  On silent white feet wending.

Surely, while she was listening on,
Fine things must to her heart have gone—
  Comfort 'gainst coming sorrow ;
Sweet hope to help her in the day
When earnest creeps into her play,
  Which must be some to-morrow.

And little as she then will know
Whence come the hopes to meet the woe—
  From what far fields they gather,
As little know we what, when sleep
Is bathing us in stillness deep,
  Comes to us from the Father.

BABY.

WHERE did you come from, baby dear?
    Out of the everywhere into here.

Where did you get those eyes so blue?
Out of the sky as I came through.

What makes the light in them sparkle and
    spin?
Some of the starry spikes left in.

Where did you get that little tear?
I found it waiting when I got here.

What makes your forehead so smooth and
    high?
A soft hand stroked it as I went by.

What makes your cheek like a warm white
    rose?
1 saw something better than any one knows.

Whence that three-cornered smile of bliss?
Three angels gave me at once a kiss.

Where did you get this pearly ear ?
God spoke, and it came out to hear ?

Where did you get those arms and hands ?
Love made itself into bonds and bands.

Feet, whence did you come, you darling
    things ?
From the same box as the cherub's wings.

How did they all just come to be you ?
God thought about me, and so I grew.

But how did you come to us, you dear ?
God thought about you, and so I am here.

———

LESSON FOR A CHILD.

ROOT met root in the spongy ground,
    Searching about for food :
Each the other went half around,
    And each got something good.

Sound met sound in the wavy air—
    That made a little to-do :

They jostled not long, but were quick and
    fair;
Each found its path and flew.

Drop dashed on drop as the rain-shower
    fell :
They joined and sunk below.
In gathered thousands they rose a well,
With a singing overflow.

Wind met wind in a garden green ;
    Both began to fret :
A tearing whirlwind arose between—
    There love lies bleeding yet.

WHAT THE BIRDS SAID AND WHAT THE BIRDS SUNG.

" I WILL sing a song :
    I'm the owl."
" Sing a song, you sing-song,
    Ugly fowl !
What will you sing about,
Night in and day out ?"

" Sing about the night :
    I'm the owl."
" You could not see for the light,
    Stupid fowl ! "
" Oh, the moon ! and the dew !
    And the shadows !—tu-whoo ! "

———

" I will sing a song :
    I'm the nightingale."
" Sing a song, long, long,
    Little Neverfail.
What will you sing about,
 Day in or day out ? "

" Sing about the light
    Gone away ;
    Down, away, and out of sight :—
    Wake up, day !
For the day is not dead,
Only gone to bed."

———

" I will sing a song :
    I'm the lark.

" Sing, sing, Throat-strong,
    Little Kill-the-dark !
What will you sing about,
Day in and night out ? "

" I can only call ;
    I can't think.
    Let me up—that's all—
    For a drink !
Thirsting all the long night—
Let me drink the light ! "

WHAT PROFESSOR OWL KNOWS.

NOBODY knows the world but me.
    The rest go to bed : I sit up to see.
I'm a better student than any of you all,
For I never begin till the darkness fall,
And I never read without my glasses ;
But that's not how my wisdom passes.

I have learning, I say—but that's not it :
I observe.   I have seen the white moon sit
On her nest, the sea, like a second owl,
Hatching the boats and the long-legged fowl !
13

When the oysters gape—you may make a
    note—
She drops a pearl into every throat.

I can see the wind : now can you do that ?
I see the dreams he carries in his hat ;
I see him snorting them out as he goes ;
I see them rush in at the snoring nose.
Ten thousand things you could not *think*,
I can write them down with pen and ink.

You see I know : you may pull off your hat,
Whether round and lofty, or square or flat,
You cannot do better than trust in me ;
You may shut your eyes in fact—*I* see.
Lifelong I will lead you, and then—I'm the
    owl—   •
I will bury you nicely with my spade and
    showl.

SIR LARK AND KING SUN.

"GOOD-MORROW, my lord !" in the
        sky alone,
    Sang the lark as the sun ascended his
        throne.

" Shine on me, my lord ; I only am come
Of all your servants, to welcome you home.
I have shot straight up, a whole hour, I swear,
To catch the first gleam of your golden
    hair. "

" Must I thank you then," said the king,
    " Sir Lark,
For flying so high and hating the dark ?
You ask a full cup for half a thirst :
Half was love of me, half love to be first.
There are some creatures as much to my
    taste,
Whose watching and waiting means more
    than your haste."

King Sun hid his head in a turban of cloud;
Sir Lark stopped singing, quite vexed and
    cowed ;
But higher he flew, thinking, " Anon
The wrath of the king will be over and
    gone ;
And his crown, shining out of its cloudy
    fold,
Will change my brown feathers to a glory
    of gold."

He flew—with the strength of a lark he
    flew ;
But, as he rose, the cloud rose too ;
And not one gleam of the golden hair
Crossed the dull depth of the unblest air ;
And his feathers felt withered and worn
    and old,
For his wings had had no chrism of gold.

Outwearied at length, and throbbing sore,
The strong sun-seeker could do no more ;
He faltered, and quivered, and dropped like
    a stone
Into his nest—where, patient, alone,
Sat his little wife on her little eggs,
Keeping them warm with wings and legs.

Did I say alone ?   Ah, no such thing !
For there was the cloudless, the radiant king.
" Welcome, Sir Lark !—You look tired : you
    see
Up is not always the best way to me.
While you have been singing so high and
    away,
I've been shining to your little wife all day."

He had set his coronet round her nest ;
Its radiance foamed on her little brown
    breast ;
And so glorious was she in russet gold,
That Sir Lark for wonder and awe grew
    cold ;
He popped his head under her wing, and lay
As still as a stone till King Sun went away.

———

THE EARLY BIRD.

A LITTLE bird sat on the edge of her
    nest ;
Her yellow-beaks slept as sound as tops;
All day she had worked without any rest,
    And had filled every one of their gibbous
      crops,
Had filled her own quite over-full,
And felt like a dead bird stuffed with wool.

" Oh dear ! " she sighed, as she sat with her
    head
    Sunk in her chest, and no neck at all—
Just like an apple on a feather-bed
    Poked and rounded and fluffed to a ball;

" What's to be done, if things don't reform ?
I can't tell where there's one more worm.

" I've had twenty to-day, and the children five
    each,
Besides a few flies, and some very fat spiders;
Who will dare say I don't do as I preach—
I set an example to all providers ;
But what's the use ?   We want a storm—
I don't know where there's a single worm."

" There's five in my crop," chirped a wee,
    wee bird
  Who woke at the voice of his mother's
    pain—
" I know where there's five."   And with the
    word
  He tucked in his head and went off again.
" The folly of childhood," sighed his mother,
" Has always been my especial bother ! "

Careless the yellow-beaks slept on—
  They never had heard of the bogy To-mor-
    row;
The mother sat outside, making her moan—
  " I shall soon have to beg, or steal, or bor-
    row;

For I never can tell the night before
Where I shall find one red worm more."

The fact, as I say, was—she'd had too many,
   And sleepless, of course, set it down to
     foresight :
A barn of crumbs, if she knew but of any !
   Could she but of the world's worm-store
     sight !
The eastern sky was growing red,
Ere she laid her wise beak in its feather-bed.

Just then, the fellow who knew of five,
   Nor troubled his sleep with anxious tricks,
Woke, and stirred, and felt alive ;—
   "To-day," he said, " I am up to six ;
But my mother feels in her lot the crook—
What if I tried my own little hook ? "

When his mother awoke and winked two eyes
   As undecided as those of a mole —
Could she believe them ? What a prize !—
   He was dragging a huge worm out of its
     hole !—
From him the old truth had its new proverb-
    form—
'Tis the early bird that catches the worm.

HYMN FOR A SICK GIRL.

FATHER, in the dark I lay,
  Thirsting for the light ;
Helpless, but for hope alway
  In thy father-might.

Out of darkness came the morn,
  Out of death came life ;
I and faith and hope, new born,
  Out of moaning strife.

So, one morning yet more fair,
  I, alive and brave,
Sudden breathing loftier air,
  Triumph o'er the grave.

Though this feeble body lie
  Underneath the ground,
Wide awake, not sleeping, I
  Shall in him be found.

But a morn yet fairer must
  Quell this inner gloom ;
Resurrection from the dust
  Of a deeper tomb.

Father, wake thy little child ;
 Give me bread and wine,
Till my spirit undefiled
 Rise and live in thine.

UP AND DOWN.

THE sun is gone down,
 And the moon's in the sky :
But the sun will come up,
 And the moon be laid by.

The flower is asleep,
 But it is not dead ;
When the morning shines,
 It will lift its head.

When winter comes,
 It will die—no, no ;
It will only hide
 From the frost and snow.

Sure is the summer,
 Sure is the sun ;
The night and the winter—
 Away they run !

INDEX OF FIRST LINES.

www.ingramcontent.com/pod-product-compliance
Lightning Source LLC
Chambersburg PA
CBHW030116030726
47498CB00007B/2406